MARIE McSWIGAN *has also written*

SNOW TREASURE

FIVE ON A MERRY-GO-ROUND

HI, BARNEY!

The game was hot and exciting

(page 37)

HI, BARNEY!

By Marie McSwigan

Illustrated by Corinne Dillon

E. P. Dutton and Company, Inc.

New York · 1946

HI, BARNEY!

CHAPTER ONE

BARNEY didn't understand the things they did at this school. He didn't like it even though Grandma called it the best in Pittsburgh. He'd been to public school in Washington and he'd rather liked that. But here at the Fortune School he felt strange and out of place.

The best he could say was that it would soon be over. It was May. Vacation would soon be starting.

It was so different from his other school. There was so much more than lessons.

Sometimes they played store or, sometimes, made paper hats. They could build blockhouses or go up and down slides. Once during the month Barney had been at Fortune they had taken a ride on the streetcar and visited a railroad yard, the most fun Barney had had in a long time.

They went to a roundhouse where engines turned around and started back where they came from. They talked to a real railroad engineer. He told them about lights and signals, about switches and sidings, and storms in the mountains.

They climbed up into his cab. One after another they took turns in his seat. They leaned out the window the way real railroad engineers do. He blew the whistle. It sounded loud inside the cab.

Back in school after that, there were all kinds of things

to do about the visit to the railroad yard. The children had to make trains out of modelling clay. In music class they made up a song about a puffing engine. And now they were building roundhouses of blocks. As if you could ever make a round house of square blocks! It seemed silly to Barney.

There was this much, though: Miss Ditman, the teacher, never kept telling them what they must do and must not do. And so, since they were allowed to do pretty much as they liked, he'd just give his roundhouse a good kick. The blocks went flying. One of them bounced into Marilyn Andrews's lap.

"Well, I like that!" She shook her long hair. "Baby! Kicks blocks around."

Some of Barney's blocks had better targets. They hit another roundhouse and almost leveled it. And this, Barney knew, was quite the worst thing you could do in the school. "Respect One Another's Work" was written on the blackboard for those who could read.

In the Fortune School the children settled their own disputes. The teacher rarely interfered. So the owner of the shattered blockhouse rose to his feet.

"Think you're a block buster, do you? Well, take that." Anthony Martin threw a handful of blocks at Barney.

Barney had scattered the ones he'd been building. He couldn't stoop to pick them up because he might be hit when he wasn't looking. On the low nursery table was a mound of wet modelling clay. He took up a handful and hurled it at Anthony. It stuck in his hair and on his face. Then Anthony began hurling clay and some of it spattered on Barney's nose.

"Children!" Miss Ditman looked up from the paper mask she was helping Lucy Lipman make.

"Barney Morrison knocked over my roundhouse." Anthony pointed at Barney.

"He threw blocks at me and I wasn't even looking at him." Marilyn was shrill and scornful.

"Why, Barney!" Miss Ditman's lips drew together. Across her forehead were lines like those on a writing tablet. "In this school we don't do things like that. We're little ladies and gentlemen who respect one another's rights."

The room quieted. The children went back to their blocks and clay, to making paper masks and bead chains. Barney felt he'd got out of it pretty easily. In any other school he'd certainly have been sent to the principal.

He wouldn't build any more roundhouses, though. He'd build an airplane hangar, a great big hangar for Spitfires and Hurricanes.

When Miss Ditman came around to see the work she stopped beside Barney.

"Yours isn't much like a roundhouse, is it?" she asked.

"It, it, it, it isn't a roundhouse." Barney sometimes stuttered when he was excited.

"Well, that's interesting. Of course, we're supposed to build roundhouses. But tell me about this hangar."

"Well, it's a Royal Air Force hangar," Barney began. "They have them all over England."

"But why a Royal Air Force hangar? Why not an American hangar for Liberators and Flying Fortresses?" she asked.

"My father's an R.A.F. pilot. A fighter pilot," Barney answered.

"Ah, that's what he's always saying! He just made that up!" In this school they didn't mind if you talked, so Anthony spoke up.

"Here're my wings. My father sent 'em from England." Barney touched the pin on his sweater, crossed gold feathers below a silver eagle and the crown of England. "My father wears this on his cap. He's a flight lieutenant. It's the same as a captain in this country."

"Ah, go on. You got that pin in Gimbel's."

"I *did not*. My father sent it from England." Barney spoke hotly. He didn't say that his father had not sent the pin to him but to his mother.

"What are you doing here then? If your father's an R.A.F. pilot, why aren't you in England with him?" Marilyn's voice was shrill and sharp.

"My grandma lives here. My mother's in Washington and I lived with her till she got a war job and sent me here."

"You don't talk like English kids," Lucy Lipman said.

"You don't say 'nipper' for child and 'cinema' for movie." Earlier that year the class had had an English "project." They still talked about it.

"I was real little when I came. Only three. I guess I didn't know any words at all. Anyway, my mother's an American. She was born right here in Pittsburgh," Barney answered.

"If Barney says his father's an R.A.F. pilot—" Miss Ditman sounded so doubtful that Barney interrupted her.

"He *is* an R.A.F. pilot, a fighter pilot. He's been flying almost five years."

"Fooey," Anthony cut in. "My father's King of Canada."

"Anthony, I'm afraid that isn't very polite—" Miss Ditman began, when Lucy Lipman interrupted.

"He's always making up things. One day he said his mother gave ten cents to the fairy to buy three cobwebs. No one would believe the things he says. Anyway, what would she want with three cobwebs?"

Barney didn't try to answer. Didn't she know he was only telling an old fairy tale? Only in this school you weren't allowed to tell fairy tales. If you called them "folk" tales it was all right. You could read them and tell them. But not if you called them fairy tales.

His father was an R.A.F. fighter pilot and a flight lieutenant. Whether they believed him or not, *he was one*. Oh, if his mother were only here! She'd know a way to make them believe it.

"I've my father's picture at Grandma's. He has his uniform on. I'll bring it tomorrow. Then you'll know," he finally ventured.

"You could have a picture but it wouldn't have to be your father," Marilyn said. "I've got hundreds of pictures of fliers; English, Polish, Russian, even Chinese fliers. My father works for a newspaper and he brings them home. I could easy pick one out and say it was my father, only I don't make up stories."

"Children, that's enough." Miss Ditman decided to put an end to the quarrelling. "It's time for the bell. Pick up your things. Barney, I'd like to talk to you. Stay after the others have gone and we'll see if we can get to the bottom of this R.A.F. business."

After the others had left, Miss Ditman sat down on a little chair beside him.

"Perhaps your grandmother would come to school some day and tell us about your father, what he does and where he is," she said. "I know you boys think a great deal about airplanes and, of course, fliers are great heroes to you. But, Barney, it's not right for you to be living a story like the one you just told the children. You are not deceiving anyone, just yourself."

There just wasn't anything Barney could think of to say to make her know he was telling the truth. Grandma would have to do it because he knew he couldn't.

She talked a little more, told him what the school was

trying to do, how it was working to make them good men and women. Then she let him go.

The other children were all out of sight by now. At the end of the walk, Nathan, the candy man, was covering his basket of candy bars, lollypops, salted peanuts, and cough drops.

"Hi ya, Nathan," Barney greeted the candy man.

CHAPTER TWO

GRANDMA refused to go to see Miss Ditman.

"If my daughter chooses to go off and marry an Englishman, I don't see why I should have to go around explaining it," she said. "I've worries enough in this big house, alone all day except for the servants."

Barney knew his grandmother was lonely. He felt sorry. But if she would only go and see Miss Ditman!

"But, Grandma, she doesn't believe me! No one in the class believes my father's an R.A.F. pilot!"

"Oh, as to that: what your father does is no concern of mine. He never asked my advice about anything he did." Grandma was knitting beside the window. The sun shone on her smooth silver hair.

"But *he is* an R.A.F. fighter pilot. He is. *You know* he is, Grandma."

"Well, I know he's doing something in the war. Just what he does isn't of great importance one way or the other."

"Oh, Grandma!" Barney was shocked. "It is important! Father's doing the most important thing in the world. He's making it safe for everybody. He's keeping the Germans out of England and America."

Mrs. Welman looked at her grandson without saying anything. The mirror over the mantle showed a beautiful room, a Persian carpet, bright chintz draperies, pots of ivy and ferns in the windows. It showed a footstool and on it a boy with straight yellow hair and wide, troubled blue eyes. The boy had knobby knees below his sand-colored shorts.

Barney repeated his request. "Grandma, if you'd only go see Miss Ditman. Tell her my father's in the R.A.F. Tell her he's one of their best pilots."

"Let her believe what she wants to. It cannot possibly make any difference." Grandma wasn't being unkind. She just didn't understand. Barney felt he could never make her know how important it was for Miss Ditman and for everyone in the school to know his father was really a flier. They *had* to know Barney wasn't just making things up. He tried again.

"Everyone laughs at me. They say I make up stories. Anthony Martin said I got these wings in Gimbel's." He fingered the pin on his pullover.

"Why, there's your Uncle Frank!" Grandma cried suddenly, and brightened as she saw a tall figure come up the walk. "He doesn't come very often, hasn't much use for us any more. He lives in that club downtown when he might just as well be living at home. My children don't care for their mother any more." She seemed so sad that Barney looked to see if there were tears behind her glasses. But no, she looked as she always did except that she was pleased over Uncle Frank's coming.

"Hi ya!" Barney ran to the door.

"Hello, fellow. Hello, Mother." Uncle Frank strode into the room and stooped to kiss his mother. "How are you, Mother?" he asked as he dropped into a deep chair and Barney went back to his footstool.

"Me? I'm always all right," Grandma answered. "Except that I get tired of sitting in this big house all by myself. Your father goes to the office in the morning and I don't see him again until dinner, and sometimes not then if he plays golf. All my children have gone their ways, you and Mary and Kitty and Bill." She named Barney's mother and his aunt and uncle.

"Well, after all, Bill's in the Navy. There wasn't much he could do about that. And Mary and Kitty have war jobs in Washington," Uncle Frank replied.

"But you're here in Pittsburgh. There's nothing to keep you at the club when you might live at home," Grandma persisted.

"How's school?" Uncle Frank turned to Barney.

"I hate school. Wish I was through college."

"What's the matter? Don't you like the kids?"

It was hard to make Uncle Frank understand. Barney tried to find words but the only ones he could think of were ones he mustn't use. He swallowed and tried again. "They're awful," was the best he could manage.

"What's the matter? They seem like a nice bunch of kids," Uncle Frank said.

"They're lovely boys and girls, and from the best homes," Grandma put in.

"They're too, too—uh, uh, important," Barney answered Uncle Frank's question.

"Too *important?*" Uncle Frank seemed surprised.

"Yes, too important. They're always making 'projects.' They couldn't build a house or a garage or a war plant. It would have to be a 'project'. Only sometimes they call them 'units.' "

"Well, if that's all that's the matter I shouldn't think you'd mind," Uncle Frank said.

"The blue team. Ugh!" Barney made a face. "The red team. Ugh! Who cares what old team wins? Those kids don't know anything, either. They don't know five times five, even if they do have measurement projects."

"How do they keep the score if they can't count? How do they know which team wins?" Uncle Frank asked.

"Oh, they know that all right. They know if anything belongs to them. They don't know numbers but they scrap over pennies."

"You make them sound like grasping little wretches." Uncle Frank stretched his long legs.

"Frank, why do you persist in living at that club?" Grandma went back to her favorite subject, her loneliness.

"Mother, I've told you any number of times," Uncle Frank answered patiently. "The house is too far from my work. When they rationed gasoline I had to move nearer the mill." Uncle Frank was production manager of Grandpa's steel works.

"Your father isn't having any trouble. He gets enough gasoline to ride to town every day. You could go with him," Grandma said.

"Dad only goes to the office. I have to go all the way out to the mill. And, Mother, I've made the change. It .doesn't seem sensible to move back."

"Here comes the mailman. Barney, run and see what he has for us." Grandma could see him from her chair in the window.

"Hi ya, Mr. Shurtz," Barney called to the letter carrier.

"Hi ya, Barney," the postman answered.

"Did you bring me anything? A letter from my—from my—" he was almost afraid to say "father" aloud.

"From your mother?" Mr. Shurtz misunderstood him. "No, I don't think she wrote this time. These are for your grandmother." He handed Barney three letters.

"I meant my father." There it was, out at last. "He's in England. He's an R.A.F. fighter pilot."

"Is that so? That's very interesting. No." He looked through another pile of mail. "He doesn't seem to have written. But maybe he will soon. I'll be watching for a letter from England."

"Oh," Barney gulped. He wouldn't want Mr. Shurtz to know it meant as much to him as it did. Mr. Shurtz was still sorting. "Here's a calendar or something for your grandmother, and the gas bill." He handed them to Barney. "Tell you what I'll do. If I have a letter from England I'll not just leave it in the box. I'll ring the bell."

"Thanks, Mr. Shurtz. Maybe you'll bring me a letter tomorrow."

"Maybe I will at that." But Mr. Shurtz didn't sound as if he thought he might.

CHAPTER THREE

WHEN Barney brought in the mail, Grandma told him to go out and play. He mustn't spend so much time indoors, she said.

There was no one to play with, though. There were no children in the neighborhood, not even a dog to make friends with.

Back in the garage Tom, the chauffeur, was washing the car.

"I'll help you, Tom." Barney took up a chamois.

"I'm not ready for that, Barney. Haven't washed the wheels." Tom's hose sloshed water over the windows and down the sides of the big black Cadillac. "How I'm going to get these tires looking the way your grandfather wants 'em, I don't know. He's cross when they don't look like new."

"Maybe you could paint 'em," Barney suggested.

"I won't have time today. He wants me to call for him at five. It's after four now," Tom said.

"What'll you do if you can't get the marks off?" Barney didn't know his grandfather very well. He didn't know how he'd be about a thing like this. His grandfather was always kind to him. He didn't say much, just made clucking noises when Barney was around. But he guessed he could get pretty angry.

"I do' know." Tom sounded as if he didn't care very much. "Guess there's nothing much your grandfather can say. I try to keep this car looking nice, but it seems kind of crazy to fuss over white-walled tires at a time like this. I like working for your grandfather. He treats me fine, gives me more money than I ever earned before. But I've got to get a war job."

"You mean that? You mean you're leaving us?" It wasn't the first time Tom had spoken of war work, but Barney hadn't really thought he meant to leave. This time he seemed to be in earnest.

"Sure I mean it. First of June I start at Dravo."

"What'll you be doing at Dravo?" Barney didn't know what Dravo was and he didn't like to ask. But Tom told him without being asked.

"Building ships, LST's and LCI's. Dravo has a big ship-yard at Neville Island."

Barney knew what LST's and LCI's were. They were the landing ships that took soldiers to Africa and Italy and to the islands of the Pacific. Some day, soon, the grown folks said, they'd be taking soldiers to France. Barney had a book of landing ships. He often made pictures of them. Now Tom was going to make them! Tom, who drove Grand-pa's car! Why, Tom came next after his father for doing something that counted!

"I like ships. I've always liked 'em." Tom was hosing the tires.

"Why don't you join the Navy like Uncle Bill?" Barney asked.

"Me? I'm too old. I was in the Navy in the last war. Submarine patrol. Wouldn't mind another hitch like that."

"Submarine patrol!" Why, Tom was more wonderful than Barney had thought. "You mean you went out and looked for subs?"

"Looked for 'em? We found 'em."

"Say, that's nearly as good as what my dad does. He's a fighter pilot in the R.A.F."

"That's what you keep saying." Tom's hose made sputtery noises.

"He flies over Germany every night. He's a fighter pilot and he 'prangs' the Germans and 'clobbers' them."

Somewhere—Barney didn't know where—he had picked up some air force language. Whether the words were English or American, he didn't know either. It was almost as though he'd made them up himself. What could be more sensible than "prang"? It just meant to smash something as if you ran a fork into a piece of squashy pie. As for "clobber," that was easy, too. When a flier clobbered an enemy ship he made spare parts of it because clobber, Barney knew, was just a lot of loose junk lying around a hangar.

"My father's been flying nearly five years," Barney went on.

"Say, that's great." But Tom didn't sound hearty. "Go into the house and ask Martha for a soft cloth, will you?"

Barney flew into the kitchen and was back with a duster. In the few seconds he was gone he had learned some news.

"Martha's leaving, too. She says she's going to a war plant."

"Yes," Tom answered, "she's going to make shells, maybe for your dad to fire."

What did he mean by that? Barney puzzled. Did he mean he really believed Barney's father was a pilot? He hadn't sounded like it before.

"You work on the fenders. You can't reach anything else," Tom directed.

Barney looked at himself in the fender. He seemed as wide as he was tall. His head was as broad as a fat boy's. But even at that, the fender was a wonderful mirror. In it he could see long cigar-shaped clouds and trees that didn't seem to grow high but grew wide with wide spreads of leaves. Between the clouds and the trees a dark thing was moving. He couldn't see it well in the black fender. He only knew something was there because it moved.

He looked up. Coming toward him was a big colored man. He wore a hat from which the brim had been cut away. Over his dark clothes hung a sack that served as an apron and fell below his knees.

"Hi ya," Barney greeted the garbage collector.

The man seemed puzzled. He hesitated a minute. Then,

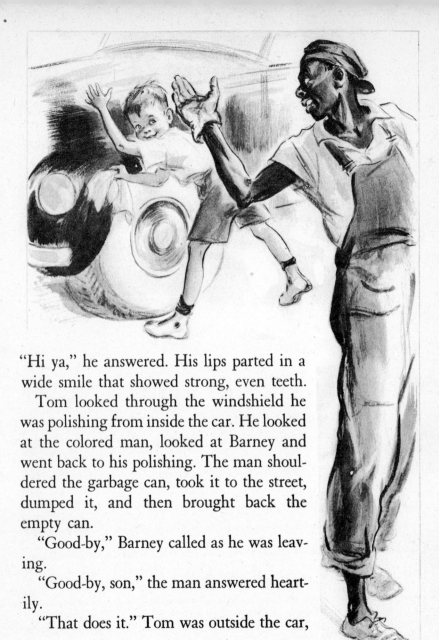

"Hi ya," he answered. His lips parted in a wide smile that showed strong, even teeth.

Tom looked through the windshield he was polishing from inside the car. He looked at the colored man, looked at Barney and went back to his polishing. The man shouldered the garbage can, took it to the street, dumped it, and then brought back the empty can.

"Good-by," Barney called as he was leaving.

"Good-by, son," the man answered heartily.

"That does it." Tom was outside the car,

examining it. Except for the marks on the tires, the car might just have left a salesroom. There wasn't a scratch nor a piece of lint. "That ought to satisfy your grandfather." He reached inside for the coat of his uniform.

"Let me go with you to get Grandpa," Barney begged.

"I'm not bringing him home. He's going to play golf," Tom answered.

"Oh." Barney swallowed. "Well, so long, Tom."

CHAPTER FOUR

WHAT to do now? It would be a long time till dinner. Barney had no idea how to fill it in.

He wandered down the driveway to the street. Across the street, Mr. Kent was working on his lawn.

"Hi ya, Mr. Kent," Barney called to his neighbor.

"Hi ya, Barney," the neighbor replied. Barney crossed the street and came up on the lawn.

"What're you doing, Mr. Kent?"

"Pulling a few weeds."

"Can I help you, Mr. Kent?"

"Sure, if you want to."

"Are the weeds bad this year, Mr. Kent?"

"We've had lots of rain. Rain makes them grow. Crab grass, too. Crab grass gets ahead of you if you don't keep pulling it."

"Your roses are beautiful, Mr. Kent. Grandma says you have the best in the city."

"Well, thank your grandma." Mr. Kent brightened at Barney's words. His roses were, indeed, fine. He had them in borders and beds and climbing around the side door. "I'll cut a few after dinner and bring them over," he added.

"That'll be fine. Grandma'll be glad. Is this a good year for roses, Mr. Kent?"

"Seems to be. Haven't any bugs yet." Mr. Kent examined the grass closely for a single weed. For all he complained of weeds and crab grass, Barney couldn't see any. Every blade of grass stood up like a bayonet at a soldier's shoulder.

"What can you do if the roses get bugs?" Barney asked.

"You just make a wash and—say, why do you want to know? What difference does it make, anyhow?"

"I just thought I'd like to know." Barney felt the red spreading over his face.

"Well, if you really want to know I'll tell you. But in all my life I never knew anyone to ask so many questions. I've been a public-school principal for ten years and in all that time I've never heard a child ask more questions. But anyway, if you *really* want to know about the bugs, I get a mixture at the seed store and use it as a spray. I just keep spraying, that's all."

"Oh." Barney couldn't think of anything else to say. He liked Mr. Kent. He liked his flowers, his big house where he lived alone except for old Minnie, the housekeeper. Martha said Mr. Kent's uncle had left him the house when he died and Minnie went along with it. Barney thought it was a good arrangement.

Searching for weeds, they covered the lawn. Since there were no weeds, they covered it fast.

A truck was coming up the street. It stopped in front of Mr. Kent's.

"There's Angelo." Barney spotted the driver, the Italian

who cut most of the lawns and trimmed most of the hedges in the neighborhood. "Hi ya, Angelo," he called.

"Hi ya, Meester Barney." Angelo's handsome brown face lighted like an electric sign. Barney liked everything about him, his kind brown eyes, his curly hair, his blue overalls, his high rubber boots. He climbed down from the truck and came up on the lawn.

"Hello, Angelo. Sit down." Mr. Kent patted a place on the grass. "I'll get us all Coca-Colas and then we'll go to the nursery for the evergreens."

"Thank you, Meester Kent." Angelo dropped down beside Barney. Mr. Kent went into the house and was back with bottles and straws. The three sat back and sipped.

"There's a bigga battle on the sea." Angelo had heard some late war news. "The Jap ships go booma, busta, bang. We sink thirteen, fourteen Jap ships."

"Yes, and we ripped Berlin again last night. We pounded it for fair," Mr. Kent added.

"My father helps rip Berlin. He goes along with the bombers and fights off the German fliers. He's an R.A.F. pilot."

"Sure. I know, I know. Your grandma, she told me," Angelo answered.

"She did?" Barney couldn't believe it. Then Grandma really knew his father was a pilot. Yet she'd told Barney that she only knew he had something to do with the war. And Angelo really believed it! You just had to hear the way he said it to know he believed it. Barney liked Angelo even better than before.

Maybe Mr. Kent would believe about his father if Angelo did. He'd try to find out.

"My father sent these wings, Mr. Kent," he said, fingering the R.A.F. pin.

"Is that so?"

Mr. Kent was funny. From the way he spoke you couldn't tell what he thought. He sounded as if he were just trying to be polite. It was hard to feel he believed Barney. You couldn't be certain the way you could with Angelo. Then Barney knew what was the matter with Mr. Kent. It was just that he didn't care.

"The R.A.F. a clean 'em up. The American fliers, too," Angelo said.

"I'll take in these bottles, then we'd better get going. 'By, Barney. I'll bring those roses to your grandmother tonight," Mr. Kent said.

Barney remained where he was on the lawn. He stayed there after the men climbed into Angelo's truck, after Angelo started the motor and drove into the driveway to turn. He watched the truck back out, make a big piece of a circle on the street. Then it came forward and was passing the house close to the curb.

"You wanna come, too?" Angelo asked Barney.

Barney wanted that more than anything else at the moment. He didn't have to answer. Angelo knew the answer.

"A'right." Angelo moved over to make room on the seat between himself and Mr. Kent. "We come back before dinner. Your grandma, I guess she won't mind I guess."

Mr. Day was getting out of his car in front of his house. He was a banker and one of the richest men in Pittsburgh. His house was the biggest and handsomest on the street. His grass was cut by his own gardener. He alone in the whole block on Bigelow Boulevard did not employ Angelo.

"Hi ya, Mr. Day," Barney called out.

"Hi ya, Barney," Mr. Day answered. Then he saw Mr. Kent and Angelo and nodded to them.

Barney felt Mr. Kent squirm on the seat beside him. He looked and saw that red was running down inside his collar. He hadn't been red sitting out there in the sun.

"Do you always greet everyone with a 'Hi ya'? Even Mr. Day?" he asked Barney.

Barney was puzzled. He knew he had done something wrong, something Mr. Kent didn't like. But he had been asked a question. He supposed he was meant to answer it, though you couldn't always tell with grown-ups. Sometimes when you answered as truthfully as you knew how, they called you "impertinent."

"Yes, I guess I do." He spoke gravely and only after he had thought it out.

"Hi ya, Henry," he called to the boy who was delivering the evening paper.

CHAPTER FIVE

THE next afternoon Mr. Shurtz, the postman, didn't even stop. He hadn't a letter for any of them. Not even a bill from the light company, nor a card from the library telling Grandma her books were overdue.

There was no one at Grandma's, however. It was Martha's day out, and Barney had been told to stay outside until Tom brought Grandma home from the Red Cross where she was making sandwiches for the blood bank.

There wasn't anyone on the street, either. Mr. Kent had set out his evergreens and must have gone away. There was no sign of Minnie, his housekeeper, nor of Blanche nor Hugh at the Tuttles'. When he went there, a black cat arched her body against his legs. "Hi ya, Blackie." Barney scratched the fur on her forehead.

He would take a walk. He didn't know Pittsburgh very well. He had lived there only a little over a month. He would like to see what was on the top of the hill, the high one where the flag waved.

Barney followed the car tracks up Centre Avenue. Up, up, the street went for a long time. He was getting tired of climbing when he came to a side street. It, too, went up a hill, but if he was going to get to the top, up where the flag waved, he'd have to climb hills.

The street made a turn and Barney turned with it. Up

here the houses weren't like the ones down where Grandma lived. Here they were mostly brown and needed paint. Shutters hung slanting from single hinges or were down on the ground, propped against the side of the house after they'd lost even the one hinge.

Around the houses were little patches of ground. There were no green lawns like Grandma's and Mr. Kent's; just plain brown ground with every here and there a scrubby tree. But there were lots of children and dogs, colored children and lean brown dogs.

"Hi ya," Barney called to the colored children.

"Hi ya," they called back.

Farther up the street the houses were neater. The shutters all hung in place and the yards had grass and some had flowers. There were no hedges or fences to keep you out, Barney noticed. Maybe colored people didn't want to keep you out. Maybe they liked to have you come in if you wanted to.

In one of the yards some children were playing a game. They stopped playing to stare at Barney.

"Hi ya," he greeted them.

"Hi ya," they called back.

Barney stopped in front of them. "What are you playing?" he asked.

A thin girl came one or two steps forward. She was a few years older than he was, Barney decided. He'd be eight next month and she couldn't be a day less than ten. She was skinny, though, about as skinny as a girl could be. Her wrists were like broom handles. She had sharp bends for elbows. But when she spoke her voice was soft and kind.

"We're playing cops and robbers," she said shyly. There was something nice about her, Barney decided. Maybe it was the way she spoke.

"Can I play with you?" he asked.

"Sure, if you want to. What's yo' name?" she asked.

"Barney Morrison."

"I'm Iwilla Hudson. These are my sisters, Tootie, Vonsie and Cleetie. And this is Poodle Davis and Bumps Bennett and Harold Paris."

"Hello, Iwilla. Hello, Tootie and Vonsie and Cleetie. Hello—" Barney was interrupted.

"Iwilla's not my whole name," the girl said. "It's short for I-Will-Arise-and-Come-to-Jesus." She seemed proud of her name.

"Why, that's a wonderful name! It must take up three whole lines on your tablet."

They laughed. Barney couldn't see why.

"Is Barney all your name? Or is it short for something else?" Poodle Davis wanted to know.

"It's Bernard, but everyone just calls me Barney." The colored children laughed at that. Soon they were laughing at almost everything he said. They seemed to think he was very funny. They laughed at him but not the way the children laughed at school.

"Come on, let's play. You be one of the robbers," Iwilla invited.

"Don't let's play cops and robbers any more. Let's play cowboys and Indians," Harold suggested.

"Well—" Iwilla looked doubtful. Then, "All right. Go get the stuff, will you, Bumps?"

Bumps darted away and was back with some chicken quills, tin cans and short stout sticks.

"We keep them under his porch," Iwilla explained. Then she turned to Bumps. "You didn't bring the beads and neckerchiefs for the cowboys. Somebody get 'em."

Harold Paris raced off and was back with loops of twine strung with spools that once held thread. With these he brought a handful of dust cloths.

"Neckerchiefs for the cowboys and drums and feathers and beads for the Indians," Iwilla explained to Barney. "You be an Indian. I'll fix yo' feathers."

"Uga-uga-uga-uga," Bumps shouted, patting his fingers over his open mouth.

"Big Chief Sock-in-the-Puss" Barney liked his feathers and spool necklace.

The game was hot and exciting. There was lots of shooting; there were many dead Indians. But Big Chief Sock-in-the-Puss couldn't be killed. He wore a pair of silver wings that kept him unharmed. At first the children didn't understand. They thought he was just showing off, spoiling their game. But he was so sure about his wings, so certain he couldn't be hurt, they stopped to have him tell about them.

"Where did you get 'em?" Vonsie wanted to know, her big dark eyes showing rings of white as they grew round with wonder.

"From my father. He's an R.A.F. pilot."

"What's an R.A.F. pilot?" she asked.

"He flies a plane for the British."

"A bomber? A Landcaster?" Harold Paris knew about the R.A.F.

"No; he's a fighter pilot. He flies a Spitfire."

"He *does*? Does he shoot down Germans?" The children were the best listeners Barney ever had.

"Hundreds of 'em." Barney wasn't so sure about that. He really didn't know much about his father. He knew only what he remembered from parts of letters his mother had read to him and from what the grown folks said. But since his father was a fighter pilot he'd *have* to shoot down German planes. Lots of them.

"He saw the King." Barney knew about this positively. It was in a letter to his mother last winter. His father had written that King George had come to his flying field and had made a speech.

The children were more interested in flying than in the King. So Barney began a long story. Part of it was true, the part he had pieced together from things he had heard. The rest of it was something he had thought about so much that he sometimes couldn't tell the real from the other.

The colored children were hanging on his every word. He was enjoying himself as never before. His story was the story of a strong man facing every kind of danger. Sometimes the wings of his plane were shot away. Sometimes he was flying over the sea without any gasoline. Sometimes he alone had to outfly ten German Messerschmitts. But no matter what the danger, some lucky thing always happened. Somehow, in some way, his father always escaped. He felt he was only starting his story when a voice called out:

"Bumps, you come fo' yo' suppah!"

"Supper time!" The children jumped up.

And Barney all at once realized it was getting late and that he didn't know where he was.

CHAPTER SIX

BARNEY felt like crying, but the son of the R.A.F.'s bravest fighter pilot couldn't do that.

The children wanted to help him find his way home.

"Where do you live?" they asked.

"Bigelow Boulevard. Forty-one thirty-one." Barney knew Grandma's address.

"Oh, I don't think that's right," Iwilla said. "Bigelow Boulevard's nothing but gasoline stations and places where they sell batteries and things for autos. There aren't any houses."

"Yeah, there're houses. Near the Bloomfield Bridge. But they're all little houses. Littler than this," Poodle said. "Do you live in a real little house?"

"No; it's pretty big. Twelve rooms." Barney felt his mouth acting funny. His lower jaw seemed to be moving up and down.

"None of 'em are that big. Five or six rooms'd be all."

Then Barney remembered he had come up a hill. All he'd have to do would be to go down the hill.

"Down that way or down there?" Iwilla pointed in one direction and then in another.

"Or down Herron, or down Bedford?" Bumps asked. This street was on the very top of a hill. From it you could go down in all directions.

"He came up that way. He must have come up Herron." Iwilla remembered seeing him come up the street.

It would soon be dark. Barney had to fight back the tears.

"If he really lives on Bigelow, it's down that way." Harold pointed.

"No, it curves around. You can get to it from Centre, too. Depends the part where he lives," Iwilla said.

"Centre. I remember. I came up Centre," Barney said. But the children didn't think that was right. And they didn't think Barney could find his way home once he got to Centre. Iwilla settled it.

"You'll have to come home with me. My father'll know how to get you home. He works for the city. He knows all the streets."

She sounded so sure of it that Barney felt better. He helped collect the things for cowboys and Indians, helped pile them under Bumps' front porch.

"You play with us again. You find your way home and come back tomorrow," Harold Paris urged.

Barney did not know what his grandmother would say about that. He would certainly like to come back, but he was troubled about getting home. He knew he'd never let go of these new friends if Grandma would let him keep them.

He said good-by to the boys, and then he and Iwilla and her sisters trudged down one street and around the corner and along another street. They came to a house and entered through a door level with the street.

In the first room were a cooking stove, a table, some chairs, a radio, and a couch.

"This is Barney. He's lost," Iwilla told her mother, who was dishing out at the stove. "Where's Dad?"

"Here." A handsome brown face showed through blue bead curtains drawn across a doorway. The man looked hard at Barney.

"Hi ya," the man said. And Barney wasn't a bit afraid. The face was kind. Though all the other colored people had looked strange to him when he first had seen them, this man didn't look strange.

"Hi ya," Barney answered when he had recovered from hearing his own greeting.

The colored man was buttoning a clean white shirt. He stepped into the room and Barney saw his well-pressed trousers, his new brown-and-white shoes. Barney felt he had seen him somewhere but he couldn't think where, unless it had been in Washington. The man smiled at him and then Barney knew where he had seen him. He remembered the smile of the garbage collector when he'd called to him yesterday while he and Tom were washing the car. No wonder he hadn't remembered him. Then he'd been wearing a hat without a brim, dark clothes, and a sack for an apron.

"He's lost," Iwilla said.

"Guess he is. He lives down on Bigelow. Saw him there yesterday."

"He said he lived on Bigelow, but the only part of Bigelow we know has service stations and little houses."

"Where he lives on Bigelow there're big houses," Iwilla's father answered.

"We'll give him supper and then you can take him home," Mrs. Hudson suggested.

"His folks're liable to be worried. I'll take him home now," Mr. Hudson answered. "Come on, boy. It won't be long before you're home. We'll take the streetcar."

Barney said good-by to the Hudsons. "Thanks for a grand time," he told them. They tittered and laughed. Iwilla, Tootie, Vonsie and Cleetie were all laughing, and so were their parents. It was such friendly laughter! Barney liked it.

It was getting dark. The street lights were on. Barney and Mr. Hudson walked down the street and made several turns. Then they went down a steep street to Centre Avenue. They had only reached the car line when a policeman stopped them.

"What's your name?" he asked Barney.

"B-B-B-B-Barney Morrison." Barney stuttered from excitement.

"Stay here with me. You, too," he told Mr. Hudson.

"I'm only taking him home. I know where he lives. I'm the sanitary man."

43

"The two of you stay right here. The radio car'll be here in a minute. It's cruising this neighborhood."

"The radio car?" Mr. Hudson seemed shocked.

"It'll take you to Number Two."

"Number Two police station?" Mr. Hudson asked. "Why should I go there? I'm only taking this boy home."

"Here's the radio car now. You'll have to go in it."

"You don't think I— You don't think I—" Mr. Hudson seemed so shocked he couldn't finish. Finally he said, "You don't think I'm kidnapping this boy, do you?"

CHAPTER SEVEN

"HERE you are, Donald. The kid you've been looking for."
The policeman stepped from the curb to stop the radio car.
He was now addressing its driver.

"The Morrison boy?" The policeman at the wheel drew
the car to a stop. Still another policeman in the car beside
him spoke.

"Seems to be the kid, all right. Hop in," he told Barney
as he reached back to open the rear door. "You, too," he
told Mr. Hudson. "He's to go, too, isn't he, Sam?" he asked
the policeman in the street.

"*I'll* say he's to go. Says he's the garbage collector and
the kid lives along his route. They'll soon check that."

"Phone the station and say we've got him, will you,
Sam?" The one called Donald spoke. He started the car.

"Where're we going?" Barney asked.

"Where would we be going but to Number Two station?" Donald answered.

Barney didn't know what to think. A ride in a radio car!
Never in his life had he expected anything as good as that!
It was almost the best thing that could happen to him. But
Mr. Hudson was sad. Barney knew he was in some kind of
trouble without knowing exactly what it was. And why
did they have to go to the police station? Why couldn't Mr.
Hudson just take him to Grandma's? Why were the police
out looking for him?

Maybe just getting lost was bad. He knew Grandma

would be angry, would scold. But he didn't see why the police would care about it. And what had Mr. Hudson done that was bad? Why, he was only taking him home!

Then he remembered a word Mr. Hudson had said—"kidnapping." Did they think Mr. Hudson was kidnapping him? Well, he'd just tell them he wasn't.

"You should let Mr. Hudson go home to his supper," he told the two policemen. "He was only taking me home. You've a car and *you* can do that."

"Won't hurt him to come with us. If he's telling the truth, he won't have to stay," the driver said.

All the time Mr. Hudson never said a word. He didn't move, either. He just sat still on the seat beside Barney.

The two in the front seat were talking to each other. Their tones were low. The two in the back seat weren't supposed to hear, but some of it they couldn't help hearing.

"Makes it worse if he *is* the garbage collector," the one beside Donald said. "Looks as if it was all planned. He saw the kid, knew the old lady was rich and just went back and got him."

"He didn't do that," Barney put in. "He didn't come to Grandma's at all. I got lost and he found me."

Ever since he had got into the car Barney could hear a sound like bees. It was as if a radio were turned on but the station wasn't broadcasting. Then all at once there was a loud "Beep" and a voice said, "WPDU, Pittsburgh 8:22. WPDU, Pittsburgh 8:22."

46

The police radio! Barney knew it at once.

"Here it is. Let's hear it," the second policeman said.

"Morrison boy reported found. Morrison boy reported found. All cars return to routine duties. All cars return to routine duties," the police radio was saying.

"Morrison boy! That's me!" Barney felt proud. Then he remembered Mr. Hudson and was sorry for him.

Barney had never been to a police station before, so he tried to see everything at once. Outside, there were colored policemen in uniform, the first he had ever seen. At the door were men in just plain clothes, detectives he knew, without being told.

They entered through a big wide door without even a screen to keep out the flies. There was a sort of hall, and after that just a big square room without furniture of any kind except benches along the walls. At one end was a brass railing and behind it a high desk on a kind of platform.

The policeman from the radio car took them up to the brass rail. Behind that and behind the desk on the platform above it, two men in blue shirts were reading comic books.

"Here they are, Lieutenant," Donald said. He whispered something and then he and the other policeman left.

"Come up here, son." The one called "lieutenant" showed Barney some steps at the side of the platform. Barney went up. "You can sit here." He pointed to a big chair, with a soft leather seat, beside his own chair. When Barney sat in it he thought of Goldilocks in the Big Bear's chair. He was too small to see over the top of the desk, to see Mr. Hudson standing at the brass rail. So he knelt up in the Big Bear's chair.

"What's your name?" the lieutenant asked him.

"B-B-B-Barney Morrison," he answered. The man beside the lieutenant put away his comics and began writing in a big book. He had been reading "Terry and the Pirates," Barney saw.

"What's your name?" The lieutenant turned to Mr. Hudson.

"Perkins Hudson," the colored man answered.

"Where do you live?"

"Sixteen, twenty-one Imalda Street." The man beside the lieutenant wrote this in the big book.

"What's your occupation?"

"Sanitary man," Mr. Hudson replied.

"Your route?" But the lieutenant didn't wait for an answer. One of the detectives was coming toward the desk and he put the next question to him. "Did you get an answer from Public Works?"

"Yeah, they've a Perkins Hudson. Been with them twelve years."

The lieutenant and the detective spoke in low tones but Barney could hear every word of it.

"Maybe he knows a collector by that name," the lieutenant said. "When we picked him up he had to think of something, so he gave that name."

"Here's the description." The detective took a card from his pocket. They read the card together and looked sharply at Mr. Hudson.

"Did you ever see this boy before?" the lieutenant asked him.

"Saw him yesterday," Mr. Hudson answered.

"Where was that?"

"At his house."

"Is that right, boy?" The lieutenant looked at Barney.

"Y-Y-Yes. I called to him and he called back. I said 'Hi ya.'"

"How do you happen to remember this boy?" The lieutenant turned back to Mr. Hudson.

"When he called to me I was glad. Most white children are afraid of a colored man. This boy wasn't. I'd hardly for-

49

get a thing like that." From the way Mr. Hudson spoke, anyone would know he was telling the truth. Barney couldn't see why the lieutenant and the detective didn't know it just from the way he talked.

"And you knew he was friendly and would come along with you? Is that it?" the lieutenant went on.

"No, no." Barney tried to make it clear. "I just got lost—" He wished someone would believe him sometimes. It was the way it was every time he said his father was an R.A.F. pilot.

Mr. Hudson answered the question that Barney had interrupted. "I didn't tell him to come with me. My daughter brought him home. He wandered into our neighborhood and didn't know how to get back where he belonged. He knew the street where he lived and the number, but she thought he'd made a mistake. She doesn't know that part of Bigelow."

"Oh, your daughter was in on this, too?" The lieutenant's voice had a whip sound.

"No; she brought him home because I'm a sanitary man and I know all the streets. She knew I could help him find his way home." If Mr. Hudson was afraid, he didn't show it. He looked straight at the lieutenant.

Some people were coming through the door.

"G-G-Grandma!" Barney jumped from the chair and was down the steps and across the floor. He buried his head in Grandma's skirt. She knelt down and put her arms around him, holding him tight. When she let him go he could see she had been crying. He could see that Grandpa looked worried and Tom did, too.

"We picked them up on Centre Avenue," the lieutenant was explaining to Grandpa. "The man says he collects your garbage and remembers seeing your grandson. He says that when the boy was lost he knew just where to take him."

"That's right, Grandpa," Barney put in. "Yesterday, when Tom and I were washing the car, he came. I was shining a fender and there was a dark thing in it and I didn't know what it was. And I looked up and it was Mr. Hudson."

"We have a Hudson in the sanitary department. The description checks. But we don't—" the detective was saying when Barney interrupted.

"Tom! You were there. Why don't you say something?" He pushed away from Grandma.

"What about it, Tom?" Grandpa asked.

But Tom looked puzzled and Barney knew why. Tom was examining Mr. Hudson but he didn't seem to recognize the man who had been in the yard the day before. But Barney hadn't remembered Mr. Hudson right away either. It was not until Mr. Hudson had smiled that he'd known him. It was the clean white shirt, the pressed pants and the new brown-and-white shoes that made him look so different.

"I yelled, 'Hi ya.' Remember?" Barney reminded Tom.

"That's right. You did. I remember now." Tom's face lit up. "I was inside the car, polishing the windshield. I heard Barney yelling to someone. When I looked it was only the garbage man. I thought, 'This is a funny kid. Tries to make friends with everyone. Is he lonesome or what?'" There was no doubt in Tom's mind now and no doubt in the way he spoke.

"Then this is the man who collects garbage in your neighborhood?" the detective asked.

"That's him." Tom was certain.

CHAPTER EIGHT

GRANDPA tried to put a bill into Mr. Hudson's hand. He refused to take it.

The police offered to take him home in the radio car. He refused that, too. He said he would take the streetcar. Then Grandpa spoke up.

"Nothing of the sort. We'll take you home."

So Tom drove the Cadillac to Imalda Street and stopped in front of the Hudsons'. Barney wanted his grandparents to go inside and meet Iwilla and her family, but Grandma refused.

"Not tonight, Barney. Mr. Hudson hasn't had his dinner. He must be very hungry after working all day."

"We certainly appreciate his not stopping to eat before starting to bring you home," Grandpa said.

So they said good-by to Mr. Hudson and tried to thank him as well as they could. After he got out of the car Grandpa said he'd like to do something for him but for the life of him he couldn't think what it would be.

"I could give him a job in the mill and he'd make more money than he does now, but it would only last during the war. In the end he wouldn't be as well off as if he'd stayed with the city." But Grandpa promised he'd find a way to do something for the Hudsons, some way to let them know he was grateful.

"How did the police know I was lost?" Barney asked. "Why did they take us in the radio car?"

"When you weren't home when I got back from the Red Cross I was worried," Grandma said. "Tom and I waited and waited and it got later and later and there was no sign of you. When your grandfather got home he was very much alarmed. There was only one thing to do, ask the police to look for you."

"And that they did. And they found you," Grandpa added.

"You ought to be in bed," Grandma said. "And you're a sight. I don't know how I'll ever get you clean."

"You'd better let him sleep in the morning. He must be tired," Grandpa observed.

Barney kept waiting for a scolding but it never came. Instead, he was going to be allowed to sleep late. That meant no school tomorrow. Things were getting better and better. The afternoon with the colored children was the best fun he had had in a long time. Then came the ride in the radio car. Barney had already forgotten how frightened he had felt when he was lost.

He didn't remember much of what was said on the way home from Imalda Street. He was too sleepy. Grandma was saying something about teaching him not to wander off and something about how she was alone in the big house every day but on the only day she went out he chose to wander away.

"Shh." Grandpa nodded toward Tom as if he didn't want Tom to hear. Anyway, whether it was because of what Tom had said in the police station about Barney's trying to make friends with everyone, or what, nothing more was said about Barney's visit to the hill. The scolding he counted on never came.

*　　*　　*　　*

Barney would be eight the last Saturday in May. Grandma asked what he wanted for his birthday.

"My father and mother," he answered before he had stopped to think what he was saying.

"We ought to have a party for Barney," Grandma declared. "We can invite the children from school."

"I'd rather have Iwilla and her friends."

But Grandma seemed not to be listening.

"I don't want a party if those kids from school have to come." Barney was sure about this.

"Oh, come, Barney. You have to have someone to play with. Why, I was never so mortified in my life as when Tom said right out in the police station—" Grandma didn't finish what she was saying, but Barney knew what she meant. Tom said he had wondered why Barney tried to make friends with everyone. Was he lonesome or what? Tom had wondered.

"We'll have the children from school," Grandma went on. "And we can have Betty King and Lucille Maloney and the Fowler twins." She named the grandchildren of some of her friends. "They're lovely children," she added.

"I don't want any party if the kids from school are coming," Barney repeated. "I have to see 'em every day. I oughtn't to have to see 'em Saturday, too."

But Grandma was determined to have a party. She sent word to Miss Ditman to tell the children to come, and she telephoned invitations to the grandchildren of her friends. The house was cleaned from top to bottom. Clean curtains, clean dresser scarves, clean bedspreads. Barney had to tidy his own room, to stack up the toys in his closet and throw away a lot of things he'd been saving. A glass doorknob, a lucky stone, a G-man badge and a Junior Commando helmet all had to be thrown away for a party he didn't want to have.

After he had finished he went outside. Mr. Kent was spreading gravel on his driveway.

"Hi ya, Mr. Kent. What're you doing?"

"Just spreading gravel. Heard you got lost. Heard the radio car was out looking for you."

So Barney had to tell Mr. Kent about his visit up on the hill and about Iwilla and her friends.

"Grandma won't let them come to my birthday party."

"Well, your grandmother knows best."

"But nobody I like is coming; just a lot of snips. The kids in school and some that Grandma knows. She says they're *lovely* children."

Mr. Kent smiled. He went on with his spreading. Barney continued, "Tell you what, Mr. Kent. You come to my party. If you can come, maybe I can stand it."

It seemed such a good idea, inviting Mr. Kent, that Barney thought he would ask a few others. The next person he saw was Angelo. Angelo didn't understand what he was saying, so he kept repeating, "Saturday's my birthday. I'm having a party. You must come."

Angelo looked puzzled. Barney was about to give up when a smile broke across Angelo's face. "Yes, yes, I know. A birth-a-day. You have a party."

Then there was Mr. Day. He'd like Mr. Day to come to his party. When he asked him he accepted at once. He'd be more than happy to come, he said.

CHAPTER NINE

THE first to arrive at Barney's party were the Fowler twins, Jim and Joe.

"You'll like them," Grandma had promised Barney.

"We'll see," he told himself. He was far from sure. But here they were, in front of him. Two curly brown heads, four shiny brown eyes, two white shirts, two pairs of tan shorts. How he was going to tell them apart, he didn't know. They were as alike as new Fords.

"Hello, Barney." Together they held out right hands.

"Hi ya, twins." Barney didn't know which hand to take first so he held out both of his. The twins didn't seem to mind. He liked the Fowlers at once. Maybe the party wasn't going to be so bad. He felt pleased with himself when he found a way to tell them apart. Jim's front teeth were wider apart than Joe's.

Besides the twins and Betty King and Lucille Maloney, Grandma had asked children of other families she knew. When they were all there, there were almost as many of them as there were from Barney's school. He began to think he might like his party after all.

None of the children brought presents. Barney was disappointed about that. But Grandma hadn't told anyone it was Barney's birthday, and after she had invited the guests she told Barney he mustn't tell anyone, either. He had already told Mr. Kent and Angelo and Mr. Day, but that couldn't be helped now.

Grandma had games for them to play. Some were funny, old-fashioned games she had played when she was a little girl. Others were like the ones the children knew, except for these they had names of their own and sometimes different rules. But they tried to do as Grandma wished. They tried hard to be polite, to play her way. They were so polite they moved quietly around the living room and library. Not even "Going to Jerusalem" got them excited. Barney was no longer hopeful about the party. He didn't think his guests were enjoying it any more than he was.

When they got tired of pinning the tail on the donkey and throwing darts in der Fuehrer's face, Grandma sent them out into the garden to wait for the real "party", for the ice cream and cake.

The children from the Fortune School had things to talk about the others didn't understand. They went to one end of the garden, while the other children were at the other end. All of them stood about, talking like grownups.

"We can't have this." Grandma had seen them from the house and came bustling out. "We'll play 'Run, Sheep, Run.'"

It was a mistake to divide into teams, the one against the other. Barney knew that right then and there. But he couldn't think of a better game, and Grandma had already started them choosing teams.

The ones from the school didn't like the others, Barney knew without being told. They heard every day how much better their school was than any other school and how children who went anywhere else wouldn't have their advantages. They just looked down on children from other schools.

As for the other children, the ones Barney met for the first time that day, he didn't see how they could possibly like the Fortune School children. Even if they tried to like them, they'd be puzzled at the funny way they acted, the things they said and did. So if you started a game in which you divided into teams, there was no telling what would happen.

Marilyn Andrews was captain of the Wolves. She chose Anthony. Joe Fowler was captain of the Sheep and he took his own brother. Barney thought that, since it was his party, he'd be one of the first to be picked. He wasn't, though. He was the very last. Since he went to Fortune, he supposed he'd have to be a Wolf, though he much preferred the other children and wanted to be a Sheep. But there were twelve from the school and only ten others. To make it even, he was put with the Sheep, and he was glad to be with Joe Fowler.

"The Sheep hide and the Wolves count to a hundred by fives." That settled, Grandma went off to help Martha with the ice cream and cake.

"You *don't* count by fives; you count by tens," Marilyn

said flatly. "If you count by fives it gives the Sheep too long to hide."

"You count by *fives*. The Sheep *need* time to hide." Joe Fowler spoke for his team.

"*We* count by tens," Marilyn answered.

"Mrs. Welman said to count by *fives*." Betty King pushed back the hair on her forehead.

"Ya, ya, ya, ya," Anthony Martin mocked, his open jaw moving from side to side.

"We count by tens or we don't play." Lucy Lipman shook her corkscrew curls.

"So we don't play." Jim Fowler turned and started to walk away. A clod of grass hit him on the back of the neck.

"Who threw that?" He gathered a handful of gravel from the drive.

"I did. Want to make something of it?" Anthony's face screwed up so his eyes almost closed.

"I'll make this much of it." Jim started forward, when Anthony's elbow caught him at the neck and the two were down on the ground.

Joe Fowler couldn't stand by and let his twin take punishment. He was on top of Anthony, trying to pull him off Jim. Six arms and legs shot out and then the others joined in a free-for-all. Marilyn grabbed Joe Fowler's leg and tried to pull him off Anthony. She had to give up when she found Betty King tugging at her waist. Then Lucille Maloney took a handful of Lucy's curls and began pulling hard.

Gravel from the driveway beat against the cellar windows as the children churned it. Hair bows, Mickey Mouse watches, toy pistols, yo-yos and handkerchiefs were ground into it.

Barney didn't know what to do. He alone of all the children wasn't fighting. He supposed he should call Grandma but he couldn't do that. He couldn't be a tattle-tale. He looked around. Angelo had left the garden hose attached to the side of the house. Barney picked it up and ran to turn on the water. He'd just give them all a little ducking and maybe they would stop fighting. He turned on the water and was aiming the nozzle at his guests when it was wrenched from his hands.

"What goes on here? What gives?" Uncle Frank had just arrived on one of his visits home. He took the hose from Barney, turned off the water and threw the hose to the ground.

Except for Barney, none of the children knew he was there. They were pounding and pulling at each other without the slightest idea that a grownup was about.

"Stop it!" Uncle Frank yelled. Then the startled children let go. They scrambled to their feet and began dusting themselves, straightening their clothes. Knees were cut. Cheeks and arms were bruised. Jim Fowler had a long tear in his shirt and another in his shorts. Hair that had been neat was rumpled. Only Lucy Lipman looked the same, her stiff curls having sprung right back into place.

"What under the sun are you children trying to do? Kill each other?" Uncle Frank asked. "Barney, what did you put these kids up to?"

"I-I-I-I—" Barney didn't know how to tell Uncle Frank that he alone wasn't fighting.

"Ya, ya, ya, ya, ya." Anthony waggled his jaw at him. "You're always starting something. You kicked over my roundhouse."

Barney started to tell Uncle Frank how it all began but everyone was talking at once. No one was listening to him.

"*He* threw grass and dirt." Jim Fowler pointed at Anthony.

"*You* threw gravel," Anthony answered.

"I didn't at all. I only picked some up."

"Well, take that." Anthony swung out, but Uncle Frank was too quick. He caught him by the arm, and as he did he tore the sleeve from his shirt.

"Listen, you young hot-heads," he said to Anthony and Jim. "You two shake hands."

"I won't shake hands. He's a drip," Anthony said.

"I wouldn't touch his filthy hand," Jim declared flatly.

"Children," Grandma called from the house, "it's time for the birthday cake. Yes, birthday cake. I've a surprise for you. Today's Barney's birthday. I know you'll all be very happy for Barney's sake. And as for Barney, he's only too happy to share his birthday treat with you."

64

CHAPTER TEN

"MERCIFUL heavens!" Grandma shrieked when she came near enough to see what had happened. She looked at Anthony's torn sleeve and at the tears in Jim Fowler's shirt and shorts. She looked at the bruises and scratches and tousled heads. Then she saw the hair bows and Mickey Mouse watches on the ground. "You children look as if you'd been in a battle."

"They have," Uncle Frank said.

"Frank!" Her face lit up. "How did you get in on this?"

"I remembered it was Barney's birthday and came home. I came just in time to stop him from turning the hose on his guests."

Grandma gasped. "Barney, I never thought it of you. I never thought you'd put your guests to quarreling."

"I-I-I-I'm the only one who wasn't fighting." Barney managed somehow to get the words out.

"You'll all have to wash before you eat," Grandma told the children. "Of course, the ice cream will be melted," she added.

"You'd better separate the school kids from the others. They'll fight again," Barney warned.

But Uncle Frank was taking charge of the boys, while Martha scurried around for towels and wash cloths, and Grandma began marching the girls upstairs. Barney was sent to get one of his shirts to replace Anthony's. Meanwhile Tom was told to put away the ice cream and to blow out the birthday candles.

The guests washed and combed. They straightened ties and hair bows, and brushed shoes. By no means the tidy children who first appeared at the party, they were presentable. The worst scars of battle were worn by Jim Fowler. He had a bruise on his forehead and tears in his shirt and shorts.

The birthday cake was a musical cake. It played "Happy Birthday to You." It not only played music but kept turning around, except when you stopped it to cut it. The children decided it was exactly like a tiny merry-go-round because it kept turning around to music.

Its icing was red and white, and among its eight blue candles waved tiny American flags. The ice cream was white and with it was red raspberry ice in tall glasses on long stems. Atop each glass waved a tiny flag. There were plates of cakes and cookies and all kinds of candies. At each plate was a frilly white cup of nuts and beside it a red cracker to snap and pull and open for the printed "fortune," the paper hat and tiny favor.

The children could forget their quarrel in pulling the crackers and putting on the hats. They seemed well pleased. They admired the cake and played with the tiny hearts and slippers, horseshoes and good-luck charms. Those who could do so read their fortunes. Barney didn't need any help on his. The tiny printed slip said, "Good luck. Good news beyond your farthest dreams comes from over the water."

"From over the water." His father was over the water, over the Atlantic Ocean!

The children were still eating when their parents came to take them home. Uncle Frank took the mothers and fathers into the living room to wait while the children finished. While they were waiting he began serving cooling drinks, for the day was warm. The grownups seemed to be having a good time, because the children could hear their roars of laughter in the dining room.

"Uncle Frank's telling about the fight," Barney guessed. With the hose in his hand, ready to turn on his guests, he must have looked a little beast. But the grownups seemed to think it funny.

When the children joined their parents in the living room, they expected to be taken home at once. But the fathers and mothers didn't seem in any hurry.

"So this is Barney." Anthony Martin's mother put her arm around him. She didn't seem to mind that Anthony was wearing one of Barney's shirts because his own was torn. "I've heard a lot about you," she said. Barney winced. He guessed she had and not anything he'd want her to hear, either.

"It's his birthday. He's eight today," Grandma was saying.

"Oh, we didn't know it was Barney's birthday," Mrs. Martin replied. "Anthony would have wanted to bring a present, wouldn't you, Anthony?" But Anthony didn't say anything. He just gave a little grunt that didn't tell whether he meant yes or no.

"Happy birthday, young man." A newcomer walked into the room and across it with long steps. Under his arm was a package which he handed to Barney.

"Mr. Kent!" Barney was grateful to see someone he liked.

"I was invited to a birthday party but my invitation didn't say what time to come," Mr. Kent was explaining. "When I saw the grownups I supposed I should come, too. Anyway, I had a present and this is as good a time as any to give it."

Barney thanked Mr. Kent and stripped off the paper. The other children stood watching. In the paper was a long narrow box and in the box a ship, a low Coast Guard cutter all spick and span in its neat sea-grey.

"It's a beauty," Mr. Lipman said as Grandma began introducing Mr. Kent.

"It's sharp."

"It's keen."

"It's built."

All of the children had something to say in admiration. Even Anthony found something to say. "It's—it's all right," he finally got out.

The doorbell rang and Tom went to answer it. Through all the noise Barney could hear Tom say:

"In here, Mr. Day." And into the room stepped the banker.

"I guess you can use this." He handed Barney a package. Barney tore away the paper. It fell on the floor, and Grandma told him to pick it right up.

Mr. Day also brought a ship, a baby airplane carrier complete with planes.

"Oh, Mr. Day! It's exactly what I needed!" Barney had heard older folks say that when they got presents and now he wondered why everyone laughed when he said it.

"You'll all have to stay and have a drink with Mr. Kent and Mr. Day." Uncle Frank brought in another tray of glasses. "The birthday cake's all gone. You'll have to use this as a substitute."

When the children found they weren't to go home immediately, they wandered out into the hall and across to the library. Barney went to tell Tom to bring more ice, and he saw the Fowler boys talking with Marilyn, while Betty King and Lucy Lipman were taking turns with Lucy's yo-yo.

It puzzled him to see them all so friendly. Why, the Fortune School children were behaving just like anyone else. They were just acting like people. Barney had never seen that happen during the whole month he'd been in school.

HI, BARNEY!

Tom was busy in the dining room, so Martha gave Barney the ice to take back to the living room. When he returned, someone else had joined the party. His sunburned face looked very brown against the clean white of his collar. He wore a good dark suit. His shoes were every bit as shiny as Mr. Day's.

"Angelo!" Barney's face lit up.

Angelo beamed right back. One thing about Angelo: you could always count on his smile. When he turned it on it was like floodlights at a night baseball game. Angelo was talking:

"I come to your birth-a-day, like you say, Meester Barney. Happy birth-a-day, Meester Barney." He handed him a big flat box wrapped in plain paper, just as it had come right out of Murphy's dollar store.

Everybody in the room watched Barney open it. No one spoke. Uncle Frank stopped serving drinks to look down at the box between Barney's hands.

"Young Patriot's Invasion Set," he read aloud. Then Barney lifted the lid to see jeeps, landing ships, transports, fighters, bombers and observation planes, soldiers, sailors, Marines, Commandos—the complete gear of invasion.

"Oh, Angelo, how wonderful!" Barney had never before realized how splendid it was to own a Young Patriot's Invasion Set.

"Angelo must meet our other guests. You already know

Mr. Kent and Mr. Day." Grandma began introducing the gardener. Then Uncle Frank stepped up with a glass.

"You'll have to drink to Barney's health, Angelo," he said.

"You betcha." Angelo's voice was hearty. "Your health, Meester Barney. In Italian we say, 'Salute.' " He took a sip. "I stop my work. I go home, changa da clothes. You know why? Because in America I'm never before been invited to a birth-a-day."

CHAPTER ELEVEN

At dinner that night Barney got other presents: a baseball suit from Grandma, an air rifle from Uncle Frank, and five dollars from Grandpa. Even Tom and Martha brought gifts: a box of handkerchiefs and a fire engine.

Nothing from Mother or Dad, though. Not even a card.

Barney fought down his disappointment. It kept coming up. He loved his other presents, loved the two ships, the Young Patriot's Invasion Set, and now these wonderful things. As far as presents went, it had been every bit as good as Christmas. If only Mother and Dad had remembered his birthday! Maybe they didn't remember he was their boy any more.

Grandpa didn't play golf that day. Because it was Barney's birthday he came home to dinner. He didn't even have Tom come for him. He just rode home on the bus. He didn't seem to mind the long wait for dinner while Grandma and Uncle Frank helped Tom and Martha clear away the party.

On the table was another cake with candles, a smaller one and no flags. It was a long time before they got to it though, because so much seemed to happen.

Mr. Kent came back with more roses and Grandma had to get up from the table to thank him. Then there was a telephone call from the mill for Uncle Frank, and they had to wait for him to finish before they could have dessert. Then Henry, the paper boy, had found out it was Barney's birthday and he rang the doorbell to wish Barney good luck. Tom brought him into the dining room to say it for himself.

"Happy birthday. Here's your paper." He handed Barney the folded newspaper and was on his way out the door when Uncle Frank stopped him.

"What's your hurry?" he called after him. "Sit down. We're going to have dessert. Ice cream and cake."

Henry looked pleased. His eyes shone. So Tom brought another glass of water, a napkin and silver, and Henry took a chair beside Barney's.

There was only one thing Henry could talk about, they soon discovered. That was baseball. So Henry and Grandpa compared batting averages. They discussed all the major-league teams and some of the minor-league ones. But Grandpa gave up when Henry began telling about the Homestead Blues and the Duquesne Greys, and about sand-lot and soft-ball teams.

The telephone rang and Tom went to answer it. He surprised them very much when he returned.

"Long distance for Master Barney," he said.

"Mother!" Barney shouted into the telephone. "I thought you'd forgotten my birthday." Then he could hardly say a thing, he was so choked.

"And how is my boy?" Mother was saying, and, because he was so choked, she had to do all the talking.

"I had hoped to be in Pittsburgh today. Since it's Saturday, I thought I could get away, spend tonight and tomorrow with you, and take the sleeper back tomorrow night. But just as I was leaving, a call came through from the boss in New York. He said he was coming to Washington and wanted me to show him our new equipment. So I had to stay and show it to him.

"My present's on its way. It'll be there soon," Mother went on. "I had to send it because I've no idea now when I can come. This was the one and only week end I thought I could count on."

"Maybe you could come for Decoration Day." Barney wasn't choked any more.

"Decoration Day's like any other day in Washington. It's a day to work, that's all. I'll say this much, a surprise is on the way. You mustn't ask me about it but you'll like it," his mother said.

"A surprise! Oh, Mother!" Then, "How's Dad?"

His mother didn't say anything for what seemed a long time. There was something the matter, Barney thought. He'd said something wrong, perhaps. His mother finally answered:

"Barney, I haven't heard from him for a good while. The last letter I had was written before Easter and I haven't had anything else. But I know I'm not to worry. Nobody gets any letters out of England just now. It's a safety measure, I guess."

"I thought he might send me a letter for my birthday," Barney said.

"I'm sure he would have if he could," his mother answered.

"He's never written to me, not even once. If he'd only write to me just once! But he never has." Barney's voice had grown shrill.

"Barney, you mustn't expect your father to write to you. He has too many other things to do," Mother reassured him. "And don't forget I haven't heard from him either for a long time. But we mustn't talk any more. They don't want you to use the telephone any longer than necessary. Be a good boy. Have all my love and a happy, happy birthday. Now you'd better put Grandma on. Good-by, dear."

Grandma would be cross if Mother hadn't asked to talk to her. That Barney knew. He said good-by and went to get her. He followed her back to the telephone and stood at her side while she talked with Mother. He wanted to say good-by again. But even when he pulled at Grandma's sleeve she didn't seem to know he was there. When she finished talking she just hung up. She seemed pleased when they were back in the dining room.

"Mary says it's awfully hot in Washington," she told them when Henry stopped talking baseball long enough to take a bite of cake. "She says Kitty's just fine but she has been working day and night." It was Grandma's chief regret that Barney's mother and aunt were in Washington and not with her in Pittsburgh.

"Mother said she was coming for my birthday but a man came from New York and she had to stay there," Barney told them.

"Why do Mary and Kitty insist on staying in Washington when it's so hot? It isn't as if either of them had to work," Grandma said.

"Maybe they follow the Washington Senators." Henry's mind, ever on baseball, named the American League club. Uncle Frank choked and coughed and almost spilled his coffee.

"No, I don't think the Senators keep them in Washington," he sputtered.

"Frank, why don't you stay here tonight?" Grandma asked. "It's Saturday. You don't have to go to the mill tomorrow."

"Well, maybe I will." Uncle Frank wiped his eyes.

"Why don't you give up your club and come live here?" Grandma went on.

Uncle Frank didn't say anything until Tom had brought him fresh coffee. And now he was carefully measuring sugar for it. "Well—" he began. But Grandma interrupted.

"It's quieter than downtown, with all those noisy streetcars and automobiles."

"You'd hardly say it was quiet around here. Not with Barney about to turn the hose on his guests and start a riot. But maybe I will come back, sometime." Uncle Frank drank his coffee.

CHAPTER TWELVE

THAT night Grandma had a speical-delivery letter from Uncle Bill. He was a lieutenant in naval aviation at Hutchinson, Kansas. Now he was being transferred to Lambert Field, St. Louis. He wanted his mother to know the news at once.

"There's a training school for the Royal Air Force at Lambert," he wrote. "It ought to be fun."

And Barney's heart gave a leap at the words.

Grandma had hardly finished reading the letter when the doorbell rang. There on the porch was Aunt Kitty. She had a week off because of extra work she had done, and her office wanted her to take it before the summer vacations started.

She was the surprise Barney's mother had spoken of.

"I wanted to be home for Barney's birthday," she said. "This was the earliest I could make it."

She brought birthday presents. She gave Barney an army belt and a garrison cap; and his mother sent him a dartboard and feather darts.

After Mother and Dad, Aunt Kitty was Barney's favorite relative. She laughed all the time. Better than anyone else, better than Mother even, she knew what boys liked. Every day in Washington she had taken Barney to the drugstore for an ice-cream cone. She ate a cone, too. She enjoyed it as much as he did. She wasn't just pretending like other grownups. She never said things like, "I'll not have one now, Barney," pretending all the time she liked cones and would have one later, when she didn't mean to at all. Not Aunt Kitty. She just ordered double dips for each of them, sometimes with chocolate sprinkle and sometimes with sourballs at the bottom.

Aunt Kitty was very pretty, Barney knew. Her hair was gold and her skin was clean and white. She wore pretty dresses, too. Barney didn't know much about dresses, but he knew hers were nice. One had gold soldier buttons. One had a red Marine anchor. And her hats, he decided, were "built," meaning very fine. One was just like General Montgomery's, even to the silver thistle.

She worked for the Army ordnance and talked about colonels and two-star generals. Barney didn't know what she did, but it was something about paying people wages. The man in charge of her office was Colonel Miller, and Aunt Kitty called him a "chicken" colonel because he wore silver eagles instead of the gold maple leaves of lieutenant colonels.

Old buildings were her hobby, old houses and churches. Before the war she had been studying architecture at Carnegie Tech, across the park from where Grandma lived. But she had left school to get a job in Washington.

Every once in a while she would ask Uncle Frank for

his car, and then she and Barney would make a tour of old houses and churches.

"I've only got an A card. Twelve gallons to last until August." Uncle Frank had refused the C card he could have had for his work. He would grumble and complain to Aunt Kitty, but he generally let her have the car.

As for Uncle Frank, he slept at Grandma's the night of Barney's birthday and every night after that. Though nothing was said about it, he just moved back home. When the expressman brought his trunk and golf bag, Martha emptied the trunk, and Tom took it to the cellar and put the golf bag in the closet under the front stairs.

The only thing Barney heard about Uncle Frank's return home was something he wasn't supposed to hear. Martha was talking to Tom:

"It's that youngster that brought him back. He thinks everything he does is funny. So now he finds it more amusing here than at his club." Then she saw Barney on the back stairs and waved the broom at him.

"Run along with you. I declare, you're always the last place anyone expects to find you."

Even with Uncle Frank at home, Grandma still talked about sitting alone in the big empty house. Aunt Kitty was here, too, and she had someone to talk to.

"Frank and your father don't get home until almost seven. And Barney's in school all day," she would say.

Something else was bothering Grandma, and Barney knew what it was. And now Aunt Kitty knew it, too.

"I don't know what I'm going to do," Grandma sighed. "Tom and Martha have both given notice. Tom's going to build ships and Martha's planning to make shells."

"Why, that's great! They're going to do war work!" Aunt Kitty spoke without thinking about Grandma.

"Great?" Grandma certainly hadn't expected this from Aunt Kitty. "You call it great! But I can't do the housework. I'm too old. And I can't hire anyone, either. Nobody can get help nowadays."

Aunt Kitty seemed thoughtful. "Can't you get day help?" she asked. "I know it's hard to get that. In Washington it's all but impossible to get any kind of help. Mary and I do most of our own work."

"My daughters doing their own work!" Grandma sounded shocked. "It's bad enough that they work in offices. But housework besides—"

"Maybe you could get your laundress to come three days instead of two." Aunt Kitty returned to the problem of getting Grandma's housework done.

"No, Della has all her days taken. I know she wouldn't come three days," Grandma answered.

Barney hoped Aunt Kitty would take him to visit an old house or a church today. But no, she couldn't take any more of Uncle Frank's gasoline. She wouldn't take the Cadillac, either. "Better save the gas. Dad'll need it," she said.

"We could go on the streetcar," Barney suggested.

"Not and get back for dinner," she answered.

Across the street Mr. Kent was pulling more weeds.

"Hi ya." Barney's greeting never changed.

"Hi ya, Barney." Mr. Kent didn't look up.

"My Aunt Kitty's home for a visit," Barney said.

"Yes, I know."

"She likes to visit old houses and churches. But we can't go because of the gasoline," Barney said.

"Oh, is that so?" Mr. Kent was always very polite but he never seemed much interested.

"How's your car? You don't drive it much, do you, Mr. Kent?"

"No, not much. Why?"

"Well, I just thought that if you had gas you could take Aunt Kitty and me to see an old house or maybe a church."

"Now, look here, Barney, what is this?" Mr. Kent sat up straight and looked at him. "Did your Aunt Kitty send you over to ask me that?"

Barney felt he was getting red. "Oh, Mr. Kent, Aunt Kitty would be mortified!" He remembered how Grandma had felt at what Tom had said in the police station the night he was lost. "Aunt Kitty would just *die* if you thought she'd ask for your car. But Mother told Grandma Aunt Kitty works too hard. So she ought to get all the fun she can while she's here."

"Oh, I see." Mr. Kent seemed to think Barney had explained everything. He was silent a minute. Then, "All I've got is an old jalopy. I wouldn't ask your aunt to ride in a rattletrap like that."

"I'm sure she wouldn't mind what the car was like. Not Aunt Kitty."

Mr. Kent still hesitated. Then, "Well, if you don't think she'd mind. When would she like to go? Tomorrow?"

"Well, we really wanted to go today. But I guess tomorrow would do."

"Oh, I could never go today. I'd have to change these old work clothes and bathe and shave."

"Aunt Kitty wouldn't mind anything like that." Barney was sure of it.

"The car's filthy. I haven't had it out in a month. It would have to be washed." Mr. Kent was thinking about something.

"Maybe we could wash it now," Barney suggested. "I always help Tom wash Grandpa's car."

"Yes, we'll wash it now," Mr. Kent sighed. "But I can't go to see any old house or church today. Tomorrow we can go. I meant to do a lot of work but I guess I can put it off. You tell your Aunt Kitty I'll be over after school. And tell her she mustn't mind how the car looks. I practically never drive it any more. Haven't much use for a car."

CHAPTER THIRTEEN

'MR. KENT wants you to come for a ride with him tomorrow, Aunt Kitty." Barney was back at Grandma's.

Aunt Kitty seemed surprised. "Mr. Kent? For goodness' sake, why?"

"Oh, he just thought you might like a ride."

"But Mr. Kent, of all people! Why should Mr. Kent take me for a ride?"

"Well, he has gasoline. He never uses his car." Barney thought this as good a reason as any. He couldn't understand why Aunt Kitty was making such a fuss.

"If that's the only reason, you go right back and tell Mr. Kent I said 'No!' " She sounded cross.

"Kitty!" Grandma spoke sharply. "Mr. Kent is one of the best neighbors anyone could have. I'm not going to have him offended because you don't want to go riding with him."

"But, Mother, Mr. Kent! He's ten years older than I if he's a day. And he's a fussy old schoolteacher." Then Aunt Kitty seemed to think something was funny. She broke out laughing.

But Grandma didn't think it was funny at all, nor did Barney for that matter. Grandma just said, "Mr. Kent is a gentleman. If he wants you to go riding, you'll have to go.

I'm not going to lose his friendship because you think he's too old for you."

"But he's—" Aunt Kitty started to say something but changed her mind. "All right, Mother. If you say so, I guess I can stand it," she said instead.

"I'm to go, too," Barney added.

"*You're* to go?" Aunt Kitty was very surprised at this. "This gets funnier and funnier. But if you're to go, Barney, I won't mind so much."

Barney was glad Aunt Kitty wanted him to go.

The next day she wore the white dress with the gold soldier buttons. She had bright red shoes with only a strap in the back to hold them on. Play shoes, she called them. Grandma made Barney take a second bath and put on clean shorts and shirt. He wore the army belt Aunt Kitty gave him. Under his belt, just the way the soldiers did, he had folded the garrison cap.

"Just exactly where is this place we're going to?" Mr. Kent asked when the three of them were seated in his car.

"What place?" Aunt Kitty asked.

"We're to see some old house or church, aren't we?" Mr. Kent answered her question with one of his own.

"Not that I know of," Aunt Kitty replied. "Barney and I sometimes see old buildings, but I didn't know we were going to see one today."

"I thought there was some place you wanted to see but

couldn't because of the gasoline." Mr. Kent hadn't started the car because he didn't know which direction to take.

"Barney, what have you been telling Mr. Kent?" Aunt Kitty asked.

Barney twisted around in the seat, not knowing what to answer. Maybe the ride wasn't such a good idea, after all.

Then Aunt Kitty burst out laughing. "I see it all now. I knew Barney had something on his mind when he left the house yesterday. I didn't know what it was then but I do now." Nobody said anything so she went on. "It's awfully good of you to go to all this trouble, Mr. Kent. But now that we understand how it is we won't have to go."

Barney hadn't a thing to say to that. Neither, it seemed, had Mr. Kent. Aunt Kitty, on the other hand, could think of lots of things to say.

"Barney, I know you thought you were doing a great thing when you planned to get me a ride. But, Mr. Kent, let's get this clear. This is the first I knew Barney was back of all this."

Mr. Kent finally found something to say. "Well, I didn't understand about it either. But now that I know, I'm grateful to him for fixing it up." He turned in his seat and smiled down on Barney. Barney felt much better. Mr. Kent never smiled much, but when he did, he was ever so much better looking. His eyes seemed to take on a shine you couldn't see any other time.

"Now that we know, we don't have to go." Aunt Kitty

had her hand on the door handle and was pushing it down.

"Oh, that wouldn't be smart," Mr. Kent decided. "It's a beautiful day and all of us planned to go somewhere. What is it you wanted to see?"

But Aunt Kitty wouldn't tell, and Barney couldn't remember where it was they would have gone if Aunt Kitty had felt it right to use Uncle Frank's or Grandpa's gasoline.

"I know a place you both might like," Mr. Kent said. "Frick Woods. The squirrels eat out of your hands. You can feed the pigeons, too. And there're chipmunks all over the place."

"Oh, let's go there!" Barney was all for Frick Woods.

"We'll have to get peanuts for the squirrels." Mr. Kent didn't wait for Aunt Kitty to object. "They like hard shelled nuts best, though I don't know where you get them this time of year."

"Run back, Barney, and see if Martha has any," Aunt Kitty said surprisingly. "Maybe she's got some walnuts. She generally keeps nuts until they're so dry she has to throw them away."

So Barney climbed out and raced back to the house. When he came back he brought a paper bag. Aunt Kitty reached into the bag and drew out a handful of nuts. "Pecans, walnuts, hazelnuts, butternuts. . . ." She let them filter through her fingers back into the bag.

"Almonds, too." Barney spotted one.

"The squirrels'll like them." Mr. Kent nodded approval as he started the car. "You ought to see Mr. Squirrel's eyes when he gets a good hard-shelled nut he can bury. Everyone brings him peanuts. He likes peanuts but he doesn't trust them to last till cold weather comes and food is scarce. So he eats them as soon as he gets them. But just give him a nut, a real nut with a sound shell, and watch his eyes glitter as he turns it in his paws and tests it with his teeth and ears to make sure there are no cracks to let in moisture. If he thinks it's cracked he eats it right away."

They drove until they came to a business section. Here Mr. Kent stopped the car. "We'll get peanuts for the pigeons. Then we'll have something to eat ourselves if we get hungry. You say the nuts are pretty dry." He went into a market and came out with three bags of peanuts.

"Now we're set." He started the car. "Have you ever been to Frick Woods?" he asked Barney. "Frick Park is its right name. It's land given the city by H. C. Frick, the steel man. In his will he said it was to be left in its natural state; no automobile roads, no service stations, no hamburger stands. So they've only cleared out some brush and cut a few trails. Otherwise it's pretty much as it was in the old days when the panthers lived there . . . panthers and bears and wolves."

"Are there any panthers now?" Barney asked. "Or bears or wolves?"

"No, they've been gone a long time, a hundred years or more. But if you look hard you might see a raccoon. A boy saw one come out of the woods not long ago."

Mr. Kent seemed glad and so did Aunt Kitty. As for Barney, it was ever so much better than seeing old buildings.

CHAPTER FOURTEEN

They left the car at the foot of a path and found themselves in the woods. The path followed the side of a hill and then began going down.

It was quiet in the woods. The only sounds were those they made themselves, when one of them spoke, or a foot made a pebble slide over the hard ground, or when one of them stepped on a twig and snapped it.

Great trees held their heads high in the air. Between the trees grew shrubs and creepers.

Coming down the path to meet them was a grey squirrel. Mr. Kent saw him first. "They hardly let you get into the woods until they come looking for nuts. Here, Barney, feed this one. Get down low so he can take it out of your hand," he said.

Barney took a walnut from the bag and sat down on the path. The squirrel came running. He made long leaps in the air as if he were in too much of a hurry to wait for his feet to cover the ground.

All at once he drew to one side of the path. Here he stood on his hind legs and looked at Barney, his head cocked on one side as if he were puzzled, not sure that Barney wouldn't hurt him.

"He's just a baby squirrel. Not so wise as the old ones," Mr. Kent explained. "He isn't quite certain it's safe. But

stay where you are and he'll come. He wants that nut. As soon as he gets bold enough he'll come and get it."

Barney rattled the nut on the ground. It was his way of telling the squirrel it was a good nut with a sound hard shell, one that he could bury, a prize of a nut, in fact.

The squirrel didn't move a hair. Only his eyes shifted from side to side. Barney kept tapping the nut on the path and the squirrel got down on his four legs and ran a few steps forward. Then he became cautious again. He went over to one side of the path, to come up to Barney from there, rather than directly from the front. Again he got up on his hind legs, his forepaws crossed on his chest as if he were praying. His forelegs had bands of white like cuffs.

"He just wants to be coaxed. Come on, Mr. Squirrel. Get the good nuts." Aunt Kitty spoke softly, so as not to frighten him. "Here come others," she added. And Barney looked around to see three squirrels coming from three directions. He watched them leap through the air.

Then Barney found he was no longer holding the walnut. While his head was turned, the first squirrel had become brave and he had come up and taken it. He ran a little way to what he must have considered a safe distance. Here he stood again on his hind legs, his forepaws turning the nut over and over. All the time his teeth were testing it to make sure it was sound enough to bury in the ground for winter when food would be scarce.

With the nut in his forepaws he made Barney think of a football player with the ball. Looks like he's getting ready to kick, he thought.

The squirrel turned the nut over many more times. His ears, his mouth and his paws were all straining to find a crack. Satisfied with its soundness, he was down on the ground again, running off to bury it. But where he took it was too far for Barney to see.

"You ought to watch one of them hide a nut," Mr. Kent said. "But maybe you'll get a chance. Look! Watch that one!"

Aunt Kitty had given a hazelnut to a fat, bold squirrel who didn't even bother to run away before he began turning it over. When he was satisfied it was sound, he took it to the foot of a tree and there, beside a long sprawling root, he dropped it while he dug in the ground. He made a hole large enough for the nut and only large enough. He didn't disturb much of the earth. No big clods flew from under his fast-moving feet. Then he took the nut and pushed it the few inches to the hole and then packed mud over it. He stamped and stamped until the ground was hard and solid. Lastly he covered the spot with a leaf so that the ground looked as if it had not been broken. When they went close to examine the squirrel's work they could hardly believe the earth had been disturbed.

"Why, the little rascal!" Aunt Kitty exclaimed. "No one would ever guess he had hidden something here! Why, there's even loose dirt on the leaf to make it look as if it had been there a long time!"

"They're smart little fellows," Mr. Kent said. "They don't need schoolbooks to make them smart."

Barney saw a big old squirrel with a wide brown streak come leaping over the grass. He didn't stop for as much as a second but came right up to Barney. He took the nut without a thought of danger, and went only a few feet before he began to examine it. Then Barney saw the look in his eyes that Mr. Kent had spoken of. His eyes were like shiny, rolling balls. They glittered like tops spinning in the sun.

"Greed, pure and simple." Aunt Kitty saw the look, too. She and Mr. Kent had been busy feeding squirrels, but she looked up now and again to watch Barney. She and Mr. Kent weren't sitting on the ground, as he was, but were stooping over.

Barney found feeding squirrels was more fun than he had ever guessed. He wanted to stay right where he was and feed them forever, almost. But Mr. Kent said they should move.

"Let's find a bench and sit down. This crouching is hard on an old man," he said. So they continued down the path and this time a trail of squirrels came after them. Every time Barney looked around he could see five, six, seven squirrels. Once he counted ten.

It took a long time to reach the bench because Barney

kept stopping to hand out nuts. Sometimes he'd have to wait until a shy squirrel got over being afraid. One of the shy ones, he thought, was the first one he had fed, the one that took his walnut when he wasn't looking. He recognized him from the bands of white on what he thought of as his "arms." Now he was back, it seemed, for another nut, but he still hadn't got over being afraid. Barney could not get him to come closer.

At the bottom of the path was a clearing, and beside it, a broad walk with benches on both sides. Pigeons strutted up and down before the benches. The ground was littered with peanut shells. The pigeons were used to being fed at this place.

"Here's where we use our peanuts." Mr. Kent shelled one and tossed it to the ground.

"Uglub, uglub, uglub," the pigeons were saying.

"Sounds like someone drowning. Making bubbles as he goes down," Mr. Kent said. Aunt Kitty's laugh startled the pigeons, who took to the air with beating wings. They circled overhead for some few minutes until they thought it safe to come back down to ground.

The squirrels hadn't given up their begging. Barney, on the bench, found he wasn't alone. A squirrel ran up the curved iron frame and along the top wooden slat at the back until he was just behind him. Barney didn't offer him a nut. He wanted to watch the pigeons. So the squirrel jumped onto his shoulder and ran down his arm to the seat, where the bag of nuts lay on its side. He went into the bag, took a hazelnut and darted off.

Another, on the seat beside Barney, sat up on his hind legs and looked into his face. Barney had been shelling peanuts for the pigeons. He took up one to shell, but before he had so much as started, the nut was gone. The squirrel had taken it out of his fingers before he could crack it.

"Well, I like that! He took it before I could give it to the pigeons!" he exclaimed.

Then he saw the squirrel opening the peanut. He bit into the shell and began eating the peanut inside as Barney would eat an ear of corn.

Mr. Kent and Aunt Kitty sat on another bench and shelled peanuts which they tossed to the pigeons. The pigeons would strut up to get them and strut away, and all the time some of them would be saying, "Uglub, uglub, uglub."

Once in a while a pigeon would take to the air, and then they tossed peanuts up toward it. But the pigeons were nearly always clumsy. Only a few could catch. The others missed and the peanuts fell, to be gobbled up by the birds on the ground.

There was a newcomer. Head down, wings outspread, a bird a little bigger than a robin clung to the bark of a tree. He was no robin, though. His wings were rusty red and his little beak was curved.

Barney shelled a peanut and then broke a little piece of

it off with his thumbnail. This he threw into the air toward the tree and the bird. Out from the tree sailed the bird. His curved beak clasped around the piece of peanut.

"A thrasher!" Mr. Kent seemed excited. "See the white underbody and the brown spots! Well, I never saw the like of that! Never in these woods have I seen a wild bird like a thrasher take food from a person. Why, Barney, it's wonderful! What made you think you could feed him?"

CHAPTER FIFTEEN

So far they hadn't seen any chipmunks. Mr. Kent said they had better go and look for them.

"They don't come much to this part of the woods, or, if they do, you don't see them. They keep to themselves in the upper part. They're more timid than the squirrels. I've never been able to get one to eat from my hand."

They walked along the broad path until they came to an open grassy place closed in by hills. Where the broad path met a narrower one there were some great, round stones. They were set off the ground on piles of smaller stones, making tables which held corn for the birds.

"These old millstones make good feeding stations," Mr. Kent observed.

"Millstones? What are they?" Barney asked, so Mr. Kent explained.

"In the old days they used these stones for grinding wheat and corn."

"Should think they'd be awfully heavy to turn," Barney decided.

"You didn't turn them yourself. The water did that. Water from a stream would turn the big millwheel, and it would be hitched up so it would turn the top millstone. Below it was one that stayed still, and between the two was the corn and wheat. When the top one turned, it crushed the grain," Mr. Kent told him.

"Where'd these come from?" Barney asked. "You said this place was just the way it was when the panthers lived here."

"Yes, where did they come from?" Aunt Kitty asked.

But Mr. Kent had no idea.

"I suppose the park people put them here when they cleaned out the dead wood and made paths," he finally said.

"Yes, but where did the park people get them? They'd have to come from somewhere," Barney insisted.

"Of course, but I don't know."

The new path began to climb. They hadn't climbed very far before Barney saw what he thought was a small brown rat. It was a bright-colored rat, though. It had stripes of light and dark in its coat. A chipmunk, Aunt Kitty called it.

When Barney tried to feed it it ran away.

"They're shy little fellows. They don't tame like squirrels. Here he comes back. Try again," Mr. Kent said.

The chipmunk wanted the nut, but not from Barney's hand. He wanted it but only if he didn't have to risk his life coming close to get it. He would have liked it if Barney had thrown it. Every time Barney thought the little creature was on the point of coming to get it, he would shy away, dash off, hide under a vine or low bush.

They went on up the path, the chipmunk following from a safe distance. They came to a little splashing stream which they crossed on a low bridge of logs. They left the path to follow the stream, because Mr. Kent said it led to a waterfall. Every time Barney looked back he could see the worried little face of the chipmunk, always at the same distance.

"Throw him the nut. He's worked for it," Aunt Kitty said.

"Try again. Maybe this time he'll come," Mr. Kent suggested. So Barney got down on his haunches and once more held out the nut. But no, Mr. Chipmunk was afraid.

"The Timid Soul." Aunt Kitty recalled her favorite cartoon character. "Caspar Milquetoast. This time he's wearing a striped blazer. He has the same neat little mustache. All he needs is eyeglasses."

Barney burst out laughing at the idea of a chipmunk wearing eyeglasses. But he could see why Aunt Kitty called him the "Timid Soul." He *did* look like Caspar Milquetoast. They had the same neat whiskers, the same worried look.

The woods were thick, now they had left the path. They would have had trouble making their way if it hadn't been for the stream. It had cut its own way through the growing things. By walking along the edge, they could use the path it had made.

Barney's head hummed with a number of things. He'd have to tell Mother about the thrasher that had caught the

piece of peanut he'd thrown. And he'd tell her about the
pigeons that went "uglub, uglub, uglub, uglub"; and about
the chipmunk that looked like Caspar Milquetoast; and
about the millstones. Was no one going to tell him how the
millstones got into these woods?

The waterfall made loud noises as it splashed down its
bank. They could hear it before they saw it. When they
reached its ledge, it fell with a great splash.

The chipmunk was still following them. Barney tried
again and again to coax him to come up to him, but he
took fright and ran off. But he always came back. Barney
saw him dart off into the brush beyond the waterfall and
he tried to follow as close as he could without frightening
the chipmunk away entirely. The chipmunk ran a little
distance and Barney followed.

The woods were thick here. Barney had trouble fighting
the brush and brambles. The chipmunk had no trouble,
though. He scurried under and over the fallen tree branches
and through the roots of bushes. Barney couldn't see where
he had gone, and then he would catch the flash of his bright
body just ahead. He followed awhile longer. Then he lost
the chipmunk. He was on the point of giving up and going
back to Mr. Kent and Aunt Kitty when he saw the little
fellow jump up onto something that looked as though it
had been part of a high stone wall. From up there he looked
down on Barney.

Barney couldn't reach far enough to hand up the nut.

Weeds and vines and part of a young tree were growing out of the stonework, so he thought he could climb the wall or whatever it was. He was used to climbing. He did it on the jungle gym every day in school. With the weeds and branches and the part of the tree, he thought he could get to the top. But no, they wouldn't hold him. The weeds and vines pulled out in his hand, and the tree didn't help him much, for it grew out almost at the bottom of the stonework.

There was something about the wall, though. It wasn't a wall at all, but something that stood all by itself in the middle of the woods. Down on the ground it was wide, but it kept getting narrower and narrower until there was only a little piece of it up there where the chipmunk was.

"There's something here," he called. "Something, but I don't know what."

He waited for Mr. Kent or Aunt Kitty to answer him, but there wasn't a sound. He looked back but couldn't see either of them. All he could see was the stone thing in front of him and the green all around. He listened for voices but could only hear the rushing noise of the water.

From up above, the chipmunk still looked down. This time, Barney thought, he didn't look so worried. It was almost as if he were grinning at him. But it wasn't a friendly grin. It was the kind you'd see on Anthony's face when you'd make the wrong answer in school.

"Aunt Kitty!" he called. "Mr. Kent!" When they didn't answer he began to get frightened. Where were they, or

rather where was he? He called as loudly as he could, but he didn't think his voice sounded very loud. His knees began to wobble. He turned around to go back the way he'd come. Only which way was it? All around in every direction were green growing things and not the sign of a path.

Barney's legs didn't seem strong any more. They didn't seem to want to walk. He thought of stories he'd heard about boys lost in the woods. Was he lost? He hadn't come very far. At least he didn't think he had.

Of course he hadn't. He could still hear the water. Aunt Kitty and Mr. Kent were right there by the big splash of water. He'd try to find his way to it and there they would be. That was all there was to it.

He had to fight back the tears, though. There he was, lost again! Only this time there'd be no Mr. Hudson and no radio car. No Grandma and Grandpa and Tom to take him home.

He set out to find the waterfall, but it wasn't so easy. Every way he turned, it sounded loud. It didn't sound any louder one way than the other. He kept walking around in a little circle, listening, listening, listening. The water was—oh wait, sssssh, a minute. Listen! Listen! He heard something and it wasn't the water.

"Barney!" Aunt Kitty was calling. She sounded frightened, but he was so glad to hear her he forgot all about being frightened himself.

"Barney!" He could hear Mr. Kent's louder voice. "Yoo-hoo, Barney!"

"Here, here, here I am." He was so excited he started stuttering.

"Up, up here." Then he could see Aunt Kitty's red play shoes. He saw them before he could see the rest of her. Then she pushed aside some branches and there she was!

"Barney! I was so worried! I thought we'd lost you!" She was breathing hard.

By now Barney had forgotten he'd been afraid, too; had been ready to cry.

"It's something that's been built here," he sputtered. Then, all at once, without knowing how he knew it, he saw what the stonework made him think of. "Something like a fireplace!" He pointed to it.

From on top the chipmunk still looked down.

"Barney, I called you and called you," Aunt Kitty said. "When you didn't answer I began to be scared."

Barney was disappointed that they didn't pay any attention to the fireplace.

"I didn't hear you, Aunt Kitty. I called you, too, and you didn't answer for a long time."

"It must have been the noise of the water," Mr. Kent decided. "It's so loud you can't hear anything else." But if he had been frightened like Aunt Kitty, he didn't show it. He was examining the stonework.

"Why, how funny! A chimney!" he said. He stripped

away some brush. They could see the stones had been put together, held by mortar, and they narrowed toward the top like a giant bottle or flask.

"This is where the millstones came from." Aunt Kitty seemed to be breathing easier. Barney didn't understand but Mr. Kent did.

"Of course. It explains everything."

Barney had no idea what they meant. He finally had to ask. Being a schoolteacher, Mr. Kent liked to explain things, so he told him about this.

"This chimney means that people lived in these woods a long time ago. I didn't think they did. I don't know if anybody today knows they did. I doubt if the park people even thought much about this. They found the millstones and decided to use them for bird feeding stations but I doubt if they connected them with this."

It still wasn't very clear to Barney, but Mr. Kent was going on.

"Most anyone in town will tell you that only wild animals lived here. But this chimney was part of a house, probably the miller's house. He had his mill here, beside the stream. The mill and the house are both gone today, but nothing could destroy this old chimney and the millstones."

"Barney discovered it," Aunt Kitty said. "He nearly scared me to death doing it, too."

"This Barney's going to be a great fellow," laughed Mr.

Kent. "First he feeds a thrasher and then he discovers an old mill. This is certainly his day."

"If it hadn't been for him we wouldn't be here now," Aunt Kitty reminded him.

"Well, Barney, you managed to give us a fine afternoon. I hope you'll arrange another one soon." Mr. Kent spoke to Barney, but he was looking at Aunt Kitty.

CHAPTER SIXTEEN

THE Tuttles, next door to Mr. Day, were moving to California. When Barney heard this he went to find out about it.

He never had any trouble getting into people's houses. He simply went in through the back door. This time, however, he stumbled over a family of black cats before he could so much as close the screen door.

There were six of them. The sleek mother cat, Blackie, trailed the smoke of a black tail. Her kittens were little round black balls. One had white forepaws like boxing gloves. Another wore a patch on his chest like a catcher's pad in baseball.

Barney stepped between the kittens and made his way into the kitchen. Blackie, the mama cat, came arching her sleek back against his bare leg.

Blanche, the cook, and Hugh, her husband, were drinking tea at the kitchen table.

"Hi ya," Barney greeted them in his usual way.

"Hi ya, Barney." Hugh, the Tuttles' houseman, placed a high stool at the table for him. "Sit down," he invited. Blanche brought him a glass of milk and a plate of cookies.

In almost all the houses Barney got snacks. Sometimes he was given a piece of pie. Sometimes it was gingersnaps or animal crackers. Always there was milk or orange juice.

"When are the Tuttles going to California?" he asked.

"Tomorrow on the noon train," Hugh answered.

"Doesn't look much like moving." Barney looked around. He couldn't see any boxes or barrels of dishes. His mother had moved in Washington. He remembered how things had been.

"Oh, they're only closing the house till after the war," Blanche answered. "Mr. James'll live here when he comes back from Italy." She seemed sad.

"Are you going to California?" Barney asked.

"No, they won't be keeping house. They'll live in a hotel," Hugh answered. He also seemed sad.

Barney nibbled a cookie. "Guess you'll be looking for work," he said.

"Yes, I guess we will," Hugh answered.

"I *know* we will," Blanche added.

"These are good cookies. Did you make 'em, Blanche?" Barney asked.

"Yes, of course."

"Martha doesn't make cookies. She doesn't make cakes, either. My birthday cake came from Joyce's." Barney named the place where Grandma got her pies and cakes.

"Anyone can make cookies and cakes, too. Nothing to it," Blanche answered.

"What will you do when the Tuttles leave?" Barney went on with his questions.

"We can stay here until we find something," Hugh answered.

"We don't know what we're going to do," Blanche sighed. "No one but the Tuttles would take the cats *and I won't part with the cats.*" There was no mistaking Blanche; she meant what she said. She *wouldn't* part with the cats.

"Grandma loves cats," observed Barney. Then he wondered if this were so. But she must love cats. She had pictures of them in the den.

"Your grandma wouldn't stand for six of 'em. Mrs. Tuttle wouldn't have either, if she could have got someone else to do her work," Blanche said.

"Grandma can't find anyone, either," Barney said. "Tom and Martha are leaving tonight. Tell you what you do. You come tomorrow. We'll need someone to get dinner."

"Oh, we couldn't do that." Blanche and Hugh looked at each other across the table. Nobody said anything for a minute and then Blanche spoke. "It wouldn't take but a couple of hours to shut up the house."

"If we stay in the neighborhood we could do it any time. Put the blankets away, clean the cellar, get the gas and water turned off. We can keep the keys and anything we forget we can do later." Hugh was talking to Blanche. It was as if Barney weren't there.

"Yes, it would be convenient staying in the neighborhood." Blanche hadn't forgotten Barney, though. "More milk?" she asked. Then, "You'd better find out what your grandmother has to say to this."

"It'll be all right with Grandma. She said she didn't know what she was going to do when Tom and Martha are gone."

"What about wages?" Hugh asked.

"Tom said Grandpa paid him more than he'd ever earned before," Barney answered. That much was true. Tom *had* said that the day they'd washed the car.

"Would your grandmother put up with the cats?" Blanche asked. "No one else will. We put an ad in the paper and dozens of people called up. We thought we ought to tell them about the cats and that was the end of it. No one would take in the cats."

"Don't worry about the cats." Barney jumped down from the stool. "You come tomorrow. Those were awfully good cookies. Thanks a lot."

"You'd better ask your grandmother and then come back and tell us what she says."

"Grandma's at the Red Cross. She's going again to-morrow. But don't bother. It'll be all right."

"Do you think she really wouldn't mind the cats?" Blanche wondered.

"Oh, she likes cats. You come."

Back at Grandma's, Barney forgot to say anything about Blanche and Hugh. He was so sorry to see Tom and Martha leaving that he forgot everything else. Martha had been good to him from the first minute he came to live at Grandma's. She had given him bread and jelly. She had let him wash his hands at the sink, and never sent him out to play just to be rid of him. And Tom had chased submarines in the last war.

Tom and Martha came into the living room to say good-by. "Nobody could ever have a better boss," Tom told Grandpa.

The next day was Grandma's regular day at the Red Cross. She used to go on other days but she never missed a Thursday. With Tom and Martha gone, Aunt Kitty would stay home to let Barney in the house, so there'd be no more running away. They were to have dinner at Grandpa's club, Barney learned.

When he got home from school, Mr. Kent was on the porch with Aunt Kitty. He was showing her photographs he had taken last summer in Canada. Barney liked the pictures of the Indians and the big fish. The ones that showed only water and trees he privately considered "dopey." When he got tired of them he went into the kitchen for a glass of milk.

Blanche was already beating up a cake. Hugh was moving in their luggage, and the kittens were rolling across the floor.

"I don't know what your grandmother planned for dinner," Blanche said when she saw Barney. "I can make out, though. I found where Martha kept her keys."

"We're having dinner at Grandpa's club. Grandma said she couldn't start cooking after working at the Red Cross," Barney said.

"If your grandmother's been working all day she'll be tired. Likely she'd sooner have dinner at home than go out. I'll just go ahead and get it," Blanche answered.

Barney found a dish of canned pears and sat down at the table to eat. He was finishing when Aunt Kitty came into the kitchen for a glass of water for Mr. Kent. She all but stepped on a black tail before she saw that the floor was alive with little black bodies. Kittens everywhere she looked!

"What makes? What goes on here?" she asked. Then she saw Blanche. "Oh, I beg your pardon. I didn't know anyone was back here with Barney."

"This is Blanche, Aunt Kitty. She makes wonderful cakes. She and Hugh are going to work for us."

"Why, that's fine!" Aunt Kitty stooped down and picked up a kitten. She held him against her shoulder and began stroking him. She seemed puzzled. "Mother didn't say anything about getting another cook. Only at lunch she said she didn't know how she was going to manage."

Blanche kept beating the cake. Barney dipped up the last spoonfuls of pear juice. Nobody said anything for a minute, so Aunt Kitty went on. "Did Mother let you in?" she asked Blanche.

"Well, no, Miss Kitty. Hugh and I just came in the back way."

"It's funny I didn't hear you before," Aunt Kitty said. "Of course, I was on the porch all afternoon, so I couldn't hear anything back here." She set the kitten on the floor. Then, "Have you everything you need? Mother wasn't planning to have dinner at home tonight so there probably isn't much in the refrigerator."

"I can make out nicely, Miss Kitty." Blanche poured batter into a shallow pan. "I suppose you deal at the O.K. Market, the same as Mrs. Tuttle? I'll make out an order and Hugh can get it."

"You seem to know what you're doing," Aunt Kitty mused. "It's funny Mother didn't say anything about your coming." She filled a glass and went back to the porch to Mr. Kent. Blanche went down into the cellar to inspect provisions, and Barney was left with the cats in the kitchen.

His grandmother didn't often come into the kitchen, but tonight she had an armful of peonies to put into water. It was a large armful and Grandma was plump. When she held it in front of her she couldn't see her feet or where she was going.

She no sooner had come into the kitchen when she heard a sharp animal shriek. She had stepped on the mother cat's tail and Blackie let out a howl. Grandma was so surprised she let fall the flowers, and when she stooped to pick them up another black tail swept in front of her face. She was

startled and drew up. As she did so, she put out her foot to step and then she saw another black tail. To avoid it she made a turn that almost threw her off her feet.

"Who let these cats into my kitchen?" She sounded angry. "Shoo, shoo, shoo. Out with you." She began waving her arms. Then she got the broom and began herding the cats toward the door.

"Stop." Blanche came running up the cellar steps. "Those are my cats," she said.

"And who are you?" Grandma rested the broom to look at the strange woman.

"I'm the new cook."

"And who hired you?"

"Master Barney, there." She pointed and Grandma saw him for the first time.

"And what has Master Barney to say about it?"

"He said you couldn't get anyone to work for you. I'm a cook, a very good cook. And my husband's a trained house-man."

"But the *cats*!" Grandma seemed aghast.

"Barney said you loved cats."

"He said I *love* cats! I can't bear the sight of them. You'll have to get rid of those cats or you can't stay here."

Blanche began to cry. "I'll never get rid of the cats. I'll take my cats and I'll go. I was cooking your dinner. I knew you'd be tired after working all day. I thought you wouldn't want to go out for dinner. And what thanks do I get? You won't even wait to see if I'm a good cook. No, it's just 'you'll have to get rid of those cats or you can't stay.' "

Grandma seemed to feel sorry for Blanche. "Come, young woman, stop weeping. My servants have always been well-treated. I can't have you crying around here. But I can't live in a house with twenty cats and that *I will not do.*"

"There're only six cats." Blanche wiped her face on her apron and then took it off and hung it on the back of a chair.

"One cat or twenty, it's all the same."

Blanche started to cry again, this time with loud sobs.

"Mother, where did you get all these cats? Everywhere I step there's a cat." Uncle Frank was picking his way into the kitchen.

"Where did *I* get all these cats? Well, I like that. Barney brought in this family of cats. He also hired a cook and a houseman. But I won't live with cats, and this young woman won't work here without them." Grandma sounded cross again.

"Is that all that's the matter?" Uncle Frank answered. "I thought something terrible was happening, something really bad." He turned to Blanche. "What's the matter with the cats living above the garage? There's a whole unfinished floor up there. You go down and get the clothes basket and I'll fix your cats the snuggest quarters they've ever had. And when you get lonesome you just go to the garage and have a good visit with them."

CHAPTER SEVENTEEN

So Grandma wasn't without a cook and a houseman after all. Blanche and Hugh were soon settled in the third floor, with the cats above the garage.

Blanche was every bit as good a cook as she said she was. Grandma liked her biscuits. The whole family praised her lemon pies, her cinnamon buns and layer cakes.

At first Grandpa couldn't get used to Hugh as a chauffeur. He kept calling him "Tom." He expected him to know without being told where he wanted to go and when he was to be taken. But Hugh always answered when Grandpa said "Tom" and soon he got to know the places to go and when to start.

As for the cats, they weren't allowed in the house. They played around the yard, and when anyone went there they were almost always underfoot. But Grandma didn't spend much time in the yard, and the rest of the family, even Grandpa, thought the cats were fun.

Blanche let Barney pick one for himself. He chose the one with the white forepaws like boxing gloves. He didn't know what to call him, so Uncle Frank named him Barnacle because he dug his little claws into anything he could get hold of.

"Barnacles," Uncle Frank explained, "are little shell creatures that stick to anything they can find—the side of a ship, the piles of a dock, anything they come across. This fellow sticks, too."

After he had to look for a ladder and climb up on the garage roof to rescue Barnacle, Uncle Frank decided he was well named.

"Barnacle Bill the Sailor's his full name," he said. "In the old days sailors had to be great climbers. They had to climb the ship's rigging clear to the top. But this fellow knows more about climbing than any sailor I ever heard of."

Barnacle could climb but he couldn't always get down from the places he had climbed to. He would go to the top of the porch or garage roof and there he would meow and meow until Uncle Frank or Hugh or Angelo found a ladder and brought him down. Then he would simply curl up in whosever hand he found himself and go to sleep.

Grandpa surprised Barney by coming for him one day after school. He and Hugh were sitting in the car at the end of the walk beyond Nathan, the candy man. Barney was too surprised for his usual "Hi ya." No one had ever come to his school for him before.

"Hop in, young fellow. We're going to pay a visit," Grandpa said as Hugh opened the door for him.

"A visit? Where?" Barney was all curiosity.

"To see some friends of yours. Remember the colored man who tried to bring you home the night you were lost?"

"Mr. Hudson? Are we going to see him?"

"No, he's working. But we'll see Mrs. Hudson and the girls."

"Oh, Grandpa, how wonderful! But why are we going to see them? I've never been allowed to before."

"Well, I promised I'd do something for Mr. Hudson and his family," Grandpa answered, "but for the life of me I couldn't think what it could be. Mr. Hudson has a job. The pay isn't bad. His house isn't exactly fine, but the family likes it. The girls go to school and get fresh milk. So I couldn't think what to do."

"Oh, Grandpa, what *are* you going to do?"

"You'll see. I had to do some looking around. Ask some questions. See what would be needed. I had to get some idea about those girls and see what would be best for them."

"I could have told you about Iwilla and Tootie and Vonsie and Cleetie," Barney said.

"Yes, but you wouldn't have told me the most important things."

"What're they?" Barney asked.

"Well, I don't know whether you noticed or not but the girl, Iwilla's just about the thinnest person alive. Her elbows would jag you. She hasn't any meat on her little bones. She needs something she's not getting."

"I know she's skinny. I saw that the first day," Barney said. "But how did you know that? Did you go to see Iwilla?"

Grandpa smiled. "I paid several visits. Both her father and mother agree that the other children are thriving, but Iwilla's health isn't all it should be. They can't find anything the matter with her, either. The school doctor says it isn't bad tonsils or anything like that. They've tried giving her tonics and having her rest, but nothing seems to help. They've just about given up trying."

He sounded serious. Barney felt suddenly frightened for Iwilla.

"What are you going to do for her?" he asked.

But they were already in Imalda Street, where the Hudsons lived, and Hugh had stopped the car in front of their house.

Barney couldn't wait for Hugh to open the car door. He pulled down the handle and when it didn't move he took both hands to it. When he finally got it open he was out of the car, racing down the walk to the house.

"Iwilla!" he called. "It's me, Barney."

CHAPTER EIGHTEEN

Mrs. Hudson opened the screen door. "The girls will be home from school in a minute. Come in, won't you?" She smiled down at Barney, and then watched Grandpa come up the walk.

She didn't seem surprised to see Barney. He guessed she was expecting him and his grandfather. The three of them went into the front room and sat on dining room chairs around the table. Barney looked at the red curtains at the windows and the blue beads that hung before the door to the next room. He looked at the brown walls and the calendars with their pretty pictures of George Washington and tanks and jeeps and one that was all yellow with the sun going down into a lake.

Grandpa put his hat on one of the chairs and from his vest pocket he drew an envelope. In the envelope were papers. One of the papers had pictures of woods and water, like the ones Mr. Kent had taken in Canada, which Barney called "dopey."

There were other papers, too, and a smaller envelope with a red border. It took Barney quite some time to figure out the two long words on the envelope. Beside the words was a picture of a streamlined engine and that helped him. "Pennsylvania Railroad" he finally read.

"I think we have everything here." Grandpa put on his glasses to examine long strips of railroad tickets.

Barney was ready to ask a question when the screen door screeched and he heard a voice.

"Barney!" Iwilla burst into the room, and behind her pressed Tootie, Vonsie and Cleetie.

Faces lit like Fourth of July sparklers as the five friends met again.

The babble of greetings was cut short by Mrs. Hudson.

"Here's Mr. Welman, Barney's grandfather. Say good afternoon to him, girls," she said.

Then Iwilla bobbed a curtsey, left foot behind right and both knees bending as she spread her short skirt. Indeed, she *was* skinny. Her legs were like hockey sticks. The other girls' legs were more like baseball bats, Barney thought as he watched them bob.

Grandpa nodded to the girls. He asked about school and if they were glad it would soon be over.

"Oh," Iwilla drew in her breath. She was smiling and her eyes were shining. "We like school, but we like vacation better."

Then Grandpa turned back to the tickets in his hands.

"I'm sorry your father can't be here," he said, "but we've talked everything over and it's quite simple. Reservations have been made. You're expected on the twentieth. You'll be met at the station and taken to the camp. These are return tickets, but you won't need them because your father will bring them when he and your mother come for their vacation."

"What is it, Grandpa? What camp?" Barney asked. All the others seemed to know about it. He was the only one who didn't.

"The girls are going to camp for a month," his grandfather answered. "Then their father and mother will come up and they'll all have two weeks more. The folder here tells what each person should have; how many shorts and shirts and blankets. But Mrs. Welman is tending to that. She knows about the sizes and she's already ordered them. They'll be here any day now. She's also getting some luggage suitcases and an Army duffle bag for the blankets and bedding."

The little faces were sparkling, eyes dancing. Mrs. Hudson was also pleased. She said, "I'm sure we're very grateful. It's about the only thing Iwilla hasn't tried. She's had medicine, tonics, cod-liver oil, and just about everything we could think of. But Doctor Oliver said six weeks in the country would do more for her than all the medicine in the world."

So this was what Grandpa meant when he said he had to find out what would be the best thing for the Hudsons, for Iwilla.

"Six weeks in the country should put some fat on her bones," Grandpa said. "She'll sleep in a tent, have fresh air all the time, and eat country vegetables. With all the fresh milk she can drink, she ought to look like Billy Bounce, the fat man of the comic strips, when I was a boy."

"Billy Bounce." The Hudson girls seemed to think this funny. "Billy Bounce!" they tittered. "Iwilla should look like Billy Bounce." Little Cleetie pointed a forefinger at her sister.

"You had no need to do this," said Mrs. Hudson. "My husband said so, too. It was a very small thing he was doing, taking a lost child home. Anyone would have done that."

"It wasn't very pleasant to be mistaken for a kidnapper," Grandpa answered.

"Will they play cowboys and Indians at the camp?" Barney had lots of questions by now. He began to ask them.

"Yes, and tennis and volley ball and soft ball. There's a big lake where they can learn to swim. And they'll have canoes and rowboats and all kinds of water sports."

Grandpa took one of the folded papers and spread it out. It showed rows of tents and a big open space around a flag-pole. Some of the pictures showed people paddling canoes, and in others they were fishing from rowboats. One had two men holding a long string of fish.

"There's just about everything at Camp Winna-Wanda," Grandpa said. "You'll learn to make Indian baskets and maybe bead moccasins."

"Maybe they can make real bead chains for cowboys and Indians," Barney suggested.

"They'll learn Indian legends and beat real drums,"

Grandpa continued. "They'll sing the camp song and Indian songs. At night they'll sit around a campfire and tell stories about bears and wild cats and about hunters and wood scouts."

"Wish I could go," Barney sighed.

"The Fortune School has a camp. You can go there if you like."

"No!" Barney sounded as if he were in such pain they all turned to look at him.

CHAPTER NINETEEN

AUNT KITTY's week was almost over. Tomorrow night she would take the sleeper to Washington.

Barney was sad about her going. But he wasn't the only one who wanted her to stay. The whole family kept telling her to stay.

"But I've got to go back. I've a war job," she said.

None of them could think of anything to say to that. Even Barney couldn't think of an answer.

Mr. Kent wanted her to stay in Pittsburgh, too. "You could do war work here," he told her.

"I can't walk out on my job in Washington." She spoke in such a way that Barney knew she didn't want to talk any more about it.

She had a letter from Margie Baines, who worked in her office in Washington.

"Margie's being transferred to Pittsburgh," she said, "to the ordnance office here. She doesn't like it, either. She's engaged to a Navy lieutenant in Washington. Now she'll have to wait until the war's over before she can get married. She wants me to find her an apartment."

So Barney and Aunt Kitty went to look for an apartment for Margie. There weren't many to look at. Few of the buildings had vacancies. The two or three they saw, Aunt Kitty called "pokey."

Everywhere they went Aunt Kitty was asked the same question. "Is the apartment for you and your son?" the manager would say when he saw the two of them.

Aunt Kitty always laughed.

"No, it's for a friend in Army ordnance who's being transferred here from Washington," she explained each time.

But after seeing all the apartments that were vacant, Aunt Kitty decided Margie would have to live at Grandma's until she could find a place for herself.

Mr. Kent had been returning Barney's visits. Before Aunt Kitty came home, almost every day after school Barney went over to Mr. Kent's. But now, Barney was no sooner in the house than Mr. Kent came to see him. Sometimes he brought flowers; sometimes he brought "cokes" or cones. Once he brought a box of candy. One evening he called on the telephone to ask Barney and Aunt Kitty to come and hear his records.

"Oh, bother, I want to pack," Aunt Kitty said. "Why can't he bring his records over here and I could listen while I pack?"

"He's got rooms and rooms of them." Barney knew all about Mr. Kent's records. "All good music, too. Mostly symphonies." Barney didn't know exactly what that meant. He had seen "Silly Symphonies" in the movies, but Mr. Kent had ones you could hear. It puzzled him.

Aunt Kitty sighed. "Well, I suppose we'll have to go.

Mother won't like it if we don't. She says we mustn't offend Mr. Kent."

Over at his house, Barney had a feeling that neither Mr. Kent nor Aunt Kitty was paying much attention to the music. They weren't paying nearly as much attention as he was. For Barney, Mr. Kent played *Peter and the Wolf* and he listened for the cat, the duck, the birds, the wolf and for Peter and his grandfather.

He liked *Peter and the Wolf,* but he didn't think the others did. Aunt Kitty just sat straight in her chair and said, "It's very interesting," as if she didn't mean it. As for Mr. Kent, he didn't say anything at all.

He played his other records. He would select one, tell its name, and the three would sit without saying a word until it was finished. Then Aunt Kitty would say something like, "It's very lovely," and he would start a new one.

Except for *Peter and the Wolf* Barney didn't think much of any of it. He would have liked something more like the music they played at the circus or at the ball game. Some of Mr. Kent's records didn't even have names, just numbers. You couldn't tell what they were meant to be. When he got tired of them he went out to see what Grandma's house looked like from Mr. Kent's porch.

When he came back the music had stopped. Mr. Kent and Aunt Kitty were talking. They both sounded cross.

"Well, I can't," Aunt Kitty seemed to snap.

"You mean you won't," Mr. Kent snapped back.

"Well, then, I won't."

They looked unhappy. With Barney back in the room they both started talking to him at once. Was he sleepy? Aunt Kitty wanted to know. Did he like the radio? Mr. Kent asked. Did he have programs he heard every day?

Barney answered as well as he could. No, he wasn't sleepy. Yes, he liked "Terry and the Pirates" and "Dick Tracy" and "Superman" and "Tom Mix." Mr. Kent brought a pitcher of fruit juice and a plate of cookies. Barney told them about the comic he liked best. He'd hardly begun to tell about Barnaby and Gorgon, the dog that answered the telephone, when Aunt Kitty brushed crumbs off her skirt and jumped up.

"It's way past Barney's bedtime. The music was beautiful," she said. "Thanks ever so much for asking us over." Then she took Barney's hand, and almost before he knew about it, they were out of the door.

Something was the matter. Aunt Kitty hadn't laughed all evening. That was strange for her.

The next day was Saturday, usually the best day of the week. This Saturday, though, something was wrong.

Aunt Kitty was pressing dresses in the cellar. Barney squatted on one of the cellar steps to watch her.

"You know what I've been thinking, Aunt Kitty?"

"What, Barney?"

"It's about your—" he started to say, but she interrupted. "Oh, Barney, you, too." Her eyes were sad. It was as if he, too, were doing what everyone else had been doing, something wrong. She went on, "I know what you're going to say. You think I oughtn't to go back to Washington. Everyone says the same thing, Mother, Frank, even Mr. Kent. And now you."

Barney flushed. "Well, that's not exactly what I was going to say. What I was going to say was about your friend, Margie Baines."

"What about Margie?"

"She hasn't a place to live in Pittsburgh. She'll have a hard time finding one. And she hates to leave her Navy lieutenant."

"She'll make out." Aunt Kitty folded a pleat. "Your mother and I had a hard time finding an apartment in Washington."

"Well, she has a place in Washington. But she's coming here where she hasn't one. And you're going back to Washington."

"I don't know what you're getting at. Margie comes here and I go to Washington. What's the matter with that?"

"You work in the same office, don't you? You do the same things she does?"

"Well, yes, I guess so. Practically, anyway." Aunt Kitty had finished the dress. She hung it on a hanger and began to spread another on the ironing board.

"Well, why don't you and Margie trade jobs? You'd be

doing her war work here and she'd do yours in Washington. And she wouldn't have to hunt for a place to live."

"Why, I never thought of that! Maybe you've got something there. Maybe we could trade, at that. Let's find out." She snapped off the iron. "I'll phone her in Washington. If they need a new person here in Pittsburgh, perhaps it wouldn't matter if it were Margie or I."

Aunt Kitty called Margie by long distance. Margie was delighted with Aunt Kitty's idea. Barney could tell that from the way Aunt Kitty was talking. Then she wasn't talking to Margie any more but was waiting for someone else to come to the telephone. She turned to Barney,

"She's all a-dither," she told him. "She thinks it's the best idea in the world."

But it wasn't so simple as they'd thought. They had to ask permission of their chief, Colonel Miller, and now he was talking to Aunt Kitty. When she explained how it was and asked if they could trade jobs, he said: in the Army you did as you were told, not as you wanted. When you work for the Army you'd better work the Army way, he said.

CHAPTER TWENTY

So Aunt Kitty would have to go back to Washington after all. There was nothing anyone could do about it.

Mr. Kent wanted her to stop work. "You're a civilian. You don't have to stay. Resign and then, if you like, apply for a job here in the Pittsburgh office."

"Oh, I couldn't do that. Not without notice," she answered.

"Did you tell your colonel your mother leads a lonely life with her children so far away?" It was Grandma speaking.

Aunt Kitty looked away. She must have wanted to laugh. "Oh, Mother, you don't think that matters to the Army, do you? If the Army stopped to consider every lonely woman in America, the Germans and Japanese would have been over here years ago."

More than Mr. Kent, more than Grandma, even, Barney wanted Aunt Kitty to stay. He thought he'd had a plan, but it hadn't worked. Colonel Miller told Aunt Kitty she wasn't to change jobs with Margie Baines. He tried to think of something else but try as he would, there was nothing he could think of that would keep Aunt Kitty from going away.

There was only one good thing about it, his mother would be glad. She lived with Aunt Kitty in Washington, and she'd miss her if she stayed in Pittsburgh.

The next day was Sunday, Aunt Kitty's last day at home. Grandma asked if she should invite Mr. Kent to dinner.

"I don't know why you should," Aunt Kitty answered.

"He gets lonesome in that big house, all by himself," Grandma said.

"He doesn't have to live alone if he doesn't want to. But ask him if you like." Aunt Kitty spoke as if she didn't care one way or the other.

So Mr. Kent came to dinner and Blanche cooked a feast. She had saved red points until she was able to get a roast of beef. With it she had roast potatoes and gravy and new peas. For dessert she had baked a cake with a foamy white icing, and with it went peppermint ice cream with chocolate sauce.

At dinner Grandpa and Uncle Frank did most of the talking. The others didn't have much to say. Grandma seemed sad. Mr. Kent ate as if he were worried. Aunt Kitty and Barney kept looking at each other.

After dinner Grandma and Aunt Kitty were talking in the living room. Barney went out on the porch to look for Barnacle. He found him on the swing. Through the open window he could hear what they were saying even though he wasn't listening very hard.

"There were lots of things I meant to do while I was home," Aunt Kitty was saying. "One was to find someone for Barney to play with. I hate to go back to Washington and know he hasn't anyone but grownups. I don't know what I ought to tell Mary." She meant Barney's mother.

"I had a party for him. He all but turned the hose on his guests," Grandma said.

"Yes, I know. Frank told me about the party. One of the boys had his shirt torn off."

"Barney doesn't get along with other children," Grandma continued. "Besides his schoolmates, I had some others, lovely children. It's a week since the party and he hasn't asked about any of them."

Barney thought about this. Maybe he didn't get along with other children. He liked the Fowler twins and Lucille Maloney and Betty King. But they had lots of friends. They didn't need him. Then he thought about the Hudsons. They had lots of people to play with, too, but they liked him anyway. They seemed so glad to see him the day he went with Grandpa. No matter how many they had to play with, he was sure the Hudsons would always be glad to see him.

"Perhaps he hasn't learned to play with other children," Aunt Kitty said. "The poor little tyke's been with grown-ups all his life."

Barney snuggled Barnacle close to him. He could feel the sharp little claws digging into his neck. He didn't mind, though. It felt good holding Barnacle so close. And he'd always known Aunt Kitty understood about boys. Now that he was just getting used to her being here, she had to go away.

Tomorrow was a school day, so Barney wasn't allowed to stay up to go to the station with Aunt Kitty. The others would put her on the train.

She came up to his room to say good-by.

"What do you want me to tell your mother?" she asked.

"Ask her please if she would write to me."

"Is that all? Don't you want to send love or anything?"

"Oh, yes. Lots of love."

"Kisses, too?"

"Well, yes. And—and—"

"What?"

"We-we-well, you said what did I want to tell my mother and I thought—"

"Yes?"

"I thought—" he hesitated a long time. He wanted to say it but it just wouldn't come out.

"Tell me, Barney."

"Tell her if she would only get my father to write."

CHAPTER TWENTY-ONE

THE next day began the last week of school. Only five more days and school would be over for the year.

After that he wouldn't have to go to bed early so he could get up "bright and early," as Grandma always said when he went upstairs at night.

He wouldn't have to be bothered with "rhythms" nor "patterns." He wouldn't have to go around saying he was a train of cars when he knew he was a boy.

He wouldn't have to see Anthony for a long time. Nor Marilyn nor Miss Ditman.

There was still that week, though. In the afternoon they had arithmetic.

"Twelve ponies are frisking in a field. Six are taken back to the stable. How many are left?" Any baby would know the answer was six. Barney looked out of the window.

"The others are playing in a circle. How many—" the teacher was saying. But Barney saw something that made him forget everything else. "How many, Barney?" What she had asked he didn't know. "Seven," he answered for no reason at all except that he had to say something.

"How many, class?"

"Six," the others answered in something more like a hiss than anything else.

"Five of the ponies run to the hedge," she was saying,

and Barney had to pull his eyes away from the window. The thing he had seen was so strange he couldn't believe it was right. He wanted desperately to look again to see if it was really so. But he didn't dare. Miss Ditman had seen him the time before and that was why she asked him a question. He would have to pay attention or she'd ask him something else.

When he dared look again, whatever he had seen was gone.

There were footsteps in the hall. Then into the room came a tall man in a blue uniform. Behind him, of all people, were Mother and Aunt Kitty! Barney thought he had seen them through the window, but he couldn't believe it. But it was really true. Here they were in the schoolroom.

"Mother!" Barney was out of his chair and across the room into the arms of his mother. She knelt down and held him tight against her.

"Here's your father, Barney. He couldn't wait till school was over to see you. He made Aunt Kitty bring us here."

"Father!" Barney freed himself to look at the tall man. Then he was ashamed. He should have known it was his father from his picture. He should have guessed from the R.A.F. uniform.

"Barney!" His father held out his hand. His eyes were bright as landing lights on a plane. His hair was just the color of Barney's own and when he said "Barney" he opened his mouth and held it open just the way Barney

knew he did himself. His father was thin though, much thinner than he thought he would be. He hadn't looked thin in the picture.

The father and son stood examining each other until Barney knew by heart every detail of his father's uniform, the stripes on his sleeve, the medal on his chest and the badge on the cap in his hand. The badge he recognized at once. It was the same as his R.A.F. pin.

"H-H-How did you get here? To America? To my school?" Barney began asking. "And Mother, why is she here? And Aunt Kitty?"

"We flew here. I, from New York, and your mother and Aunt Kitty, from Washington." Barney's father was smiling all over. He smiled with his eyes and his mouth and his whole face. But Mother was explaining to Miss Ditman:

"I hope you'll forgive our coming into your class this way, but Barney's father arrived from England only today. He hasn't seen Barney since he was three years old, since the war started over there. He was so anxious to see him he wouldn't take time to come to Washington but had me meet him here. In fact, the train wasn't fast enough. We had to fly."

Barney looked at his mother and then back to his father.

"Barney told us his father was in the Royal Air Force," Miss Ditman was saying.

"Nobody'd believe me, either," he blurted out.

"I don't think I know your rank." Miss Ditman turned to Father.

"Flight lieutenant," he told her.

"What would that be in the United States service?" she asked.

"Captain, I think, in your Army; lieutenant, in your Navy. You see, the Royal Air Force is neither the Army nor the Navy but a separate branch of the service."

"Are you on leave?" she asked.

"No, on a mission. Perhaps a long one. I've been sent to the Royal Flying School at Lambert Field, Missouri."

"That's where Bill is!" Aunt Kitty spoke for the first time. And now Barney had a hard time believing it really was Aunt Kitty. Why, she had gone back to Washington only last night! And here she was in Pittsburgh again. It didn't make sense to Barney.

However, as to that, nothing made sense. He was so staggered at seeing his father at last that he could hardly believe it was he. He couldn't take in the meaning of what he had just said. It was a long time before he realized his father's work had brought him to this country. But Miss Ditman was speaking.

"Perhaps you'd say a few words to the class."

"Goodness, no; I'm no talker," Father answered, smiling apologetically.

"Oh, Father, *please*." The way Barney said it must have made his father know that that was what he wanted more than anything else in the world. His father started to shake his head but stopped. He looked at Miss Ditman, looked at Barney, then, "Well, if you think there's anything I could say that would interest the class . . ."

"Oh, Father!" Barney was shocked. Nothing would interest it more.

"There really isn't much to say," Father insisted.

The children had been seated in a half circle around Miss Ditman. Now they hitched forward their chairs, eager to hear him. Even Anthony seemed eager.

"I'm the new administration officer at St. Louis," he said, and Barney's heart sank. His father didn't speak at all the way he thought he might. He felt anxious and a little disappointed because his father's words were kind of dry and it seemed as if he were going to talk of just everyday things.

He went on, "My work will largely be on paper. I'll assign replacements and all that sort of thing. I may do a little teaching, but no more combat flying." From the way he spoke, you couldn't tell whether he was glad or sorry he wouldn't be fighting any more.

"Barney said you flew over Germany," Lucy Lipman said.

"Yes, of course. That was our job. We had to go up and fight off the German fighter planes so our bombers could get through to their targets."

"And you 'pranged' them and you 'clobbered' them, didn't you?" Barney felt he had to say it.

His father smiled. "You've picked up some Royal Air Force talk. Yes, we 'pranged' and we 'clobbered.' "

"How many did you shoot down?"

"Twenty for certain. Some others, of course, though we don't count them unless we see them fall."

Miss Ditman got chairs for Mother and Aunt Kitty and for herself. They joined the semicircle of children.

"Perhaps you'd tell us about one of your—what do you call them, 'runs'?" Miss Ditman asked.

"We call them sweeps."

"Oh, tell us about one! Tell us about a sweep!" All the children spoke together.

"I'll tell you about one that a member of my fighter group went on," Barney's father said. Barney felt easier in his mind. He'd been afraid his father wouldn't tell much about anything, only about the paper work he was going to do. And here he was about to tell a story.

CHAPTER TWENTY-TWO

This is the story Flight Lieutenant Morrison told the second grade of the Fortune School:

"Our bombers went on a sortie to get a tank works in northern France. The fighters went along to keep them from aerial attack. It was the Wednesday before Easter, if you want to know the exact date, and the middle of the afternoon when real trouble began for one of the fighter pilots we shall call David.

"David came out of a cloud to find a German Messerschmitt coming right at him. He turned back into the cloud to escape, and found a second German ME right in his path. He was in a bad spot, without a friendly aircraft anywhere near.

"He did the only thing he could do, what any of you would do. That was to make the best of a bad situation. He went after the second ME, and he and the German pilot shot it out. By and by David was lucky enough to see he had hit the German. He had the satisfaction of seeing the ME go down. He thought he was very fortunate, thought his own plane hadn't been touched. So now for the other one.

"What he had done to the second ME made the pilot of the first one pretty mad. He came head-on after David, and by this time David had begun to realize he hadn't been so lucky after all. He saw plenty of trouble right in his own ship before he could so much as train his guns on the first plane. But he *did* get him in his sights and shot him down. Then he realized his Spitfire was literally shot to pieces.

"His feathering mechanism was out of commission. His propeller was windmilling and his rudder cables were shot away. But none of it mattered because his engine was useless. He had to bail out.

"He thought he was a gone goose. The Germans have all of France, you know, and he had to land in enemy-held territory. It was broad daylight and the Germans couldn't miss him. He landed near a woods but knew the woods couldn't hide him long.

"You can imagine his surprise when he loosened his parachute straps and saw a small boy no bigger than Barney, here. The boy had a dirty, streaked face. He wore ragged overalls and was barefooted. But he was a sturdy little fellow who held himself like a man.

"He stood guard over a big wicker basket with hinged lids, the kind we use for picnics in England.

" 'Hurry to take off the uniform and put on these,' he said in English. Out of the basket he had taken some clothes: a coarse woolen coat, a pair of baggy pants, and a pair of wooden shoes such as the people of Europe have been wearing these war years. With them went a cloth cap with a visor, the kind worn by cricket—I mean baseball—players.

145

" 'Why are you speaking English?' he asked the boy. 'This is France, isn't it?'

" 'I speak English because the American fliers cannot speak French,' the boy answered. 'The British can speak some—but not the Americans. So I had to learn. But you must hurry,' he urged. 'You must give me the uniform, complete with papers and all marks of identity. Money you can keep. You have the francs, is it not? I thought so. The francs you keep. Everything else you give to me.'

"David changed into the coarse peasant clothes. Then he reached into his uniform pocket and brought out the chocolate and toffee he always carried. The boy's eyes glittered when he saw the candy, but he put it into the basket along with the uniform.

" 'Now the parachute,' the boy said. So they gathered and stuffed it into the basket and carried it to the foot of a tree.

" 'We'd better hide it in the bushes,' David suggested.

" 'No need for that,' the boy answered.

"David began practicing walking in the wooden shoes. The boy stood still to listen. After a time David felt he could manage the shoes. He waited for the boy to take him somewhere, but the boy stood quite still. David didn't know what he ought to do, but he knew he mustn't stay where he was. But still the boy made no motion to go. He was worried about the basket. But when he looked at the tree the basket was gone.

"He started to go, but the boy told him to stay.

" 'It is not safe to go this minute,' he said.

" 'My name is David. What's yours?' he asked when he had recovered from his surprise at seeing the basket gone.

" 'Gervais.' The way the boy answered, David could tell he didn't want to talk.

"He wasn't sure that the boy's name *was* Gervais. He knew it was a common name for boys in France. Although it might very well be his name, there was something about the way he spoke that made David think it was not. If it was not his real name, David knew why he had chosen to tell him it was. He recognized in the boy a member of the French underground. If he wanted to keep his name secret, he surely must be allowed to do so.

"Gervais seemed to be waiting for some signal. If it came or not, David could not tell. David neither saw nor heard anything, but perhaps Gervais did, because of a sudden he said, 'We can go now.'

"They began following a trail through the woods, Gervais leading the way.

" 'How did you find me so quickly?' David asked.

" 'I was on the watch. We watch all the time. We look for English and American fliers.' The boy spoke coolly. He was civil and only that. David felt he didn't like him very much. He wondered what he had said or done to make Gervais speak so shortly. Then he knew. Gervais had been trained to watch his answers, trained not to speak without thinking, not to talk much at all. Although David didn't know a great deal about children, he found this boy's behavior strange. It was anything but childlike.

" 'I'm grateful you were watching,' he said.

" 'Oh, you fell in my part. We have the woods divided. Over there is Antoin's. Beyond the church is René's. From the slope to the church is mine. If the Germans got you first, I alone would be to blame.'

" 'But you have helpers. The basket was gone!' David couldn't keep from trying to find out how this strange work was carried on.

" 'Those are not for the rescue of fliers,' Gervais answered. 'They are only for taking the baskets.' He spoke with pride. David knew he was one of a few who had been chosen to guide the airmen. The others had important tasks, too, but Gervais and a few others had the most important ones.

"All at once Gervais stopped dead in his tracks. For himself, David couldn't hear a thing. But Gervais heard something, for he put his finger to his lips for silence. 'The Germans have found where you landed. They were quick this time. Do not say anything but come as fast as you can.'

"David did not have to be told to hurry, but the shoes were clumsy. He kept sloshing up and down in the mud of a spring thaw.

"They were coming to the edge of the woods. A wagon

track grew out of the ground and they walked along it. After a while Gervais slowed his pace.

" 'We never walk fast if we think Germans might be about,' he said in a low voice. David felt uncomfortable. So the Germans could be close at hand.

" 'No more English,' the boy commanded. 'I'll do all the talking.'

" 'But I speak French,' David answered.

" 'You do?' Gervais seemed puzzled. Then, 'But you are English! I remember the uniform. I did so want to save an American.' He seemed disappointed.

"David had to laugh. 'You'd think the R.A.F. didn't count for anything!"

" 'But I *have* saved English fliers, three of them, and not even one American. My brother and I have a wager. Fifty centimes for the first American.'

" 'You speak very good English.' David tried to make him feel less unhappy in his disappointment.

" 'I speak German, too. It is a gloomy tongue, but I had to learn it.'

" 'But why, for goodness' sake?' David asked him.

" 'We children, alas, have to spend much time with the Germans. We must know what they say so we can tell our parents if it is anything they should know.'

"David had to admire how well this French underground was built. It really trained its workers. They had to learn their jobs, just as if they were working in factories or in machine shops. This little boy of eight or so had to know English and German. He probably had to know all sorts of other things.

"Well, David decided, nothing was going to stop a people that determined. Nothing could keep down a people so clever as to give small boys work that grownups dared not do. David looked at the boy with admiration. He looked at the trees and the distant hills and up at the sky of France."

CHAPTER TWENTY-THREE

NOBODY in the class said a word. Flight Lieutenant Morrison went on:

" 'The Germans know a British pilot was shot down. It is not safe to go to the village or to a farmhouse,' Gervais told David. They were still following the wagon track, but the trees were fewer. Soon they would be out of the woods.

" 'Why not stay here in the woods then?' David asked.

" 'They know you fell near the woods. They will beat every bush, look up every tree.'

" 'I see. I can't go into the village nor to a farm. Where, then, are you taking me?'

"Ahead was a stone wall cut by a rough wooden gate. Over the gate was a crucifix. A cemetery.

" 'The Germans took our gate. Father Ferrand had the men make this one,' Gervais explained.

"The graves were like shrines. Some had pictures of the dead in round glass cases like crystals on the faces of clocks. Other graves had candles or lamps, each with a glass chimney to shield the flame. A wide flagged walk through the graves brought them to a low flight of steps. They went up the steps and across a stone porch into an almost dark church.

"David's shoes clattered horribly on the stones that did not end with the porch but continued into the church. In-

side he could see little more than the red sanctuary lamp
burning in front of the altar. As his eyes grew more accus-
tomed, he saw what he thought were mummies. All round
the church in front, on the two sides, perhaps even behind
him, were forms covered with dark cloth. Then he remembered. It was Holy Week. During the two weeks before
Easter all the statues in Catholic churches are covered with
purple as a reminder of Christ's passion and death.

"In front of the altar, Gervais knelt and crossed himself
and began to pray. David dropped down beside him, grateful for his own deliverance from the murderous Messerschmitts and for his escape thus far from the Germans on
the ground below. He, too, began to pray.

"He prayed his heart out in thanksgiving. He knelt there
unmindful of the boy, of the strange little dark church, of
the enemy-held land. He didn't remember ever praying
like that before. He had no idea how long he was there in
front of the altar. He said, 'Thank you, God,' in as many
different ways as he knew how. He was saying it again and
praying for further deliverance when he felt eyes on
him.

"He tugged at Gervais's sleeve, nodding toward the dim
corner from which he felt the eyes, even if he could not
see them.

"Gervais crossed himself again and got up. He was going
toward the shadow, when there was a clatter of wooden
sabots such as the clatter David's had made.

"Someone was coming toward him. All he could see was a white, white face. As it got nearer he saw that the figure was tall and seemed to be wearing a long dark dress. On its arm was a swathe of dark cloth.

" 'It's our priest, Father Ferrand,' Gervais explained. Then he turned to the priest. 'He speaks French, Father.'

"David found himself looking into the bluest eyes he had ever seen. The eyes seemed to search him for quite some time. Then a hand went out and took his own.

" 'My son, thank God we found you.'

"What David mistook for a long black dress was the cassock of a Catholic priest. The cloth on his arm, he could now see, was the same purple that covered the statues.

"David started to speak but the priest cautioned silence.

" 'The Germans saw you fall. They want you very much for a prisoner. They won't be long in coming for you. They'll even look for you here because the church is no longer a sanctuary. Until now, we French priests have been able to hide your fliers in our confessionals. That has been discovered. We have had to think of something else.' He extended his arm with the purple cloth.

" 'One thing is good,' he went on, 'the time of year, the passiontide. In all our churches our statues are covered with purple. Until tonight, when it will be safe to take you away, you will be a statue covered with purple. You must keep very still, stand in your niche along with Our Blessed Lady, St. Michael and the others.'

"He motioned David to come with him. In one of the walls was an empty niche.

" 'Our St. Denis was destroyed in one of the most senseless of bombings. In 1940, when we were still in the war, the Germans dropped bombs that didn't hurt anything but the ground they hit. The percussion, however, annoyed our St. Denis, and he fell out of his niche. We have not had the money to replace him. For today, you can be St. Denis. Take off your shoes and climb up there.' The priest handed him the purple cloth. 'If you put this part in front of your face, you will find slits that may help you breathe more easily. They may even let you see a little.'

"David climbed into the niche and put the cloth over his head. It fell to his feet, to the base of the niche. Then Father Ferrand began pinning it in folds. He must have dressed statues hundreds of times, for he knew just where to pin. David knew that, when he was through pinning, the folds would be tucked in as neatly as were those of the other statues.

"The boy, Gervais, stood back to get the effect. His ears, David thought, were sharper than other people's, for he seemed to hear something.

" 'They come, Father,' he warned.

" 'It is good enough.' The priest regarded his work calmly. 'Come, then; we pray the litany.'

"The priest and the child knelt in front of the altar. *'Sancta Maria,'* the priest chanted in Latin.

" '*Ora pro nobis*,' Gervais chanted back.

" '*Mater Dei*,' Father Ferrand went on.

"David could hear the sound of boots on the stone floor. Then a streak of light showed as the door opened a crack. Through the crack came a steel helmet. The wearer was uncertain. He seemed about to withdraw. Then the door opened wide and he seemed to be pushed into the church, along with a German corporal and two other privates. Rifles rested on shoulders. On the rifles were bayonets.

"The men walked stiffly to the front of the church. Before the altar they parted, two going to each side.

"They dared not interrupt the priest at his prayers, dared not come between him and the altar. There were some things, David realized, that even German soldiers dared not do.

"Like many other European churches, this one had no pews. It had only tiny wicker kneelers and behind these no aviator could hide. There was no place for the Germans to look, save in the confessionals, and these were soon examined.

"One of the soldiers stopped before a draped statue. His bayonet made a screech as it slit the cloth. Then the tip of the bayonet rang against the stone of the statue.

" 'Put up those bayonets.' Father Ferrand rose from his knees and turned toward the soldier. 'You would even destroy the house of God.'

" 'We are looking for an escaped English aviator,' he

answered. He had not dared to move after the priest's command. His bayonet cut the air in front of him.

" 'Have you seen an English aviator?' The corporal, too, had stopped where he was.

" 'Fight your war on the battlefield. Leave the house of God in peace.' The priest spoke with authority. 'We will now go back to our prayers,' he said to Gervais.

" '*Regina coeli*,' he was chanting.

" '*Ora pro nobis*,' Gervais answered.

"The corporal was undecided. 'He must have come this way. There's nowhere else for him to have gone,' he said.

"If Father Ferrand heard him, he gave no sign. He simply went on with his litany. The soldiers made a great stir of looking in the sacristy or robing rooms. Then they clattered their way into the baptistry. They found no English aviator. They withdrew from the church.

"Father Ferrand had finished his litany and began a singsong. David couldn't imagine what language he was singing; he knew it wasn't Latin. It could have been French. It was French. It went:

" 'And now will the good St. Denis listen to our prayer!' St. Denis! He was standing in the niche of St. Denis. The words were meant for him. The priest had said something, and to make sure David understood, he was repeating it.

" 'When darkness falls upon the land, then let it please the Almighty to send his messengers. Deliver thy servants,

O Lord, from this land of tears. Deliver them from the sight of the enemy and thus may they find peace in thy protection. Amen.'

" 'Amen,' answered little Gervais.

" 'When darkness falls upon the land.' When it was safe at night the priest would send for him."

CHAPTER TWENTY-FOUR

THERE was more to Flight Lieutenant Morrison's story. Nobody so much as moved a finger when he stopped to get his breath. He continued:

"David heard Father Ferrand and Gervais leave the church. It was darker than ever with the covering over his face. He had only his ears to tell him if the Germans would come back. But Father had said to stay there until he would be 'delivered.' He had no choice but to go on being a draped statue.

"He couldn't tell about the time. He knew that at six o'clock it was customary for bells in church steeples to ring out the Angelus, the call to sunset prayer. But the Germans had taken away the cemetery gate and doubtless they had taken the church bell also. In any event no Angelus rang out over his head.

"Since it was Wednesday of Holy Week there was a service in the church that night. The service was called the *Tenebrae* or Shades of Darkness, in memory of the sufferings of Christ. During the singing of the *Tenebrae* all the candles would be put out, except one that symbolized Christ. Even that one would be hidden so its light could not be seen.

"The choir chanted the solemn lament of the passion. There was no organ or any other kind of music save the deep wail of sadness, suffering and death. As the candles went out, the dim church grew dimmer and dimmer. Still the lament went on in its sad, slow way.

"When the singing reached a certain pitch there was sudden silence. Then the last candle was taken away and the church was in darkness. Then it was that David felt a tug at his purple drapery. It fell loose around his ankles. Hands must have unpinned him because he was free of the cloth.

" 'St. Denis, step down from your pedestal,' a voice whispered. He was guided by hands. In the black he jumped to the floor. 'Your shoes. Put them on when we stop.' In his hands were the wooden sabots. He was steered into the center of the church.

"The candle, that had been hidden, was now brought back to the altar. Others were lit, one by one. Soon David could make out the people around him, old women in black, old men with wrinkled dark faces. Of the very few young men, two leaned on crutches.

"The congregation was still singing. 'Sing!' the man commanded David. Without knowing the Latin words or even the tune, David found he was singing.

"After the service, Father Ferrand stood at the door to say good night to his people. He did not even look at David. David knew it was the last time he would ever see the brave priest, but he did not dare to stop and say his thanks. Beside the priest was his altar boy in cassock and surplice. David could hardly believe that this was the ragged boy who had found him in the woods.

"Outside, an almost full moon destroyed the blackout. David had counted on the blackout to save him from the Germans, but the night was bright. And the Germans patrolled the roads, stood guard over the bridge of the Oise, continued their search for an English pilot. Any strange face would be challenged. But the brightness of the Eastertide moon did not help them. David's companion was skillful in finding shadows when they were near.

"David knew the man simply as Louis. He and Louis went back into the woods and through it for a long time until they came to a deep, rutted road. They followed it long after the moon had gone down. They left the road only a few minutes before the first streaks of light started a new day.

"They walked along a narrow road a few minutes until they came to what David found to be a worked-out coal mine. Louis simply pushed in some boards and into the mine they went.

"Inside it was safe to show a light, and Louis had an electric torch—you Americans call it a flashlight. With the flashlight they found their way to a room dug out of the rock. Here was a pile of straw for a bed, blankets, matches, a candle and, best of all, a loaf of bread, cheese and a bottle of wine. David fell on the food. He had not eaten for almost a whole day.

" 'It was not possible for you to eat earlier,' Louis said. 'We had to reach here before day and we only just did that.'

"David was too busy to answer. The man, Louis, went on:

" 'You must stay here until you are sent for. It may be days or it may be weeks. You will not be forgotten. I will bring you food, a passport, German cards of travel. Under no circumstances will you move from here. All that we tell you, you must do. If you do not obey, it may be death for Father Ferrand, for myself, for perhaps hundreds of others. For ourselves, it doesn't matter. We know the risk and we take it. But if you are captured and the Germans find out who helped you, it will mean the lives of other British and American aviators who fall in France. We French have to stay alive to help you airmen.'

"David understood. He promised complete obedience in everything. In fact, he had no wish to do but what these men directed. He tried to thank Louis, but Louis shook off his thanks.

"David lived in that abandoned coal mine for two weeks. Every day Louis brought him food, boiled potatoes and smoked dried fish and, now and again, milk. Once he brought a single egg, of which he seemed proud. Once he was prouder than ever. He brought something so precious he carried it on a plate covered with a fringed napkin.

"It was a wizened, dry orange. The French Forces of the Interior had wrecked a German train from Spain. The cargo fell to the wreckers. This particular orange, Louis explained, had passed through many hands, had been a long time getting here. That is why it was so dry and wizened.

"One day Gervais accompanied Louis to the mine. They wheeled in a bicycle. 'This you will ride as long as the directions tell you. They will also tell you how the bicycle is to be taken off your hands and perhaps given to another.'

" 'Where are the directions?' David asked.

"In reply, Louis unscrewed the end of one of the bicycle's handle bars. In the hollow of metal tubing was a coil of paper. On the paper in fine writing were detailed instructions. They told how every hour of his time must be spent for the next several days until he would arrive at the farm of a certain Monsieur X.

" 'Monsieur X will start you for Monsieur Y. Here is your *carte d'identite*. Other papers you will get from Monsieur Z, transit papers for Spain, a Portuguese *visé*. Do exactly as it says and all will be right.'

"David tried to give him the French francs he carried. Louis waved them away. 'You will need these and more. Monsieur Y or Monsieur Z will give you what more you need.'

"Gervais refused to take any of them either. 'There is no need,' he said. 'Today I have everything I want. At sundown last night an American was shot down. He fell in my territory. I got him only seconds before the Germans came. We had to hurry but we succeeded.' His eyes shone.

"David congratulated him on this most wonderful thing of all, an American rescue.

" 'He gave me chewing gum,' Gervais said. And David resolved then and there that if he ever made any more sweeps over France he would carry gum.

"Gervais not only refused David's francs but insisted on giving him a present instead, an Iron Cross, the German award for bravery.

" 'Where did you get it?' David asked him.

" 'My brother could not pay the fifty centimes for getting the first American. He gave me this, instead.'

" 'But where did he get it?'

" 'The Germans pinned it on him for a joke. They think he helps them. They teach him the German way, to salute and say "Heil Hitler." Father Ferrand says it is not wrong for him to do these things. Father has great plans for Henri. He's ten. He can do so much.'

"David had his own idea about the plans for Henri, and about the time when the English and Americans would land in France. Perhaps the priest encouraged the boy to make friends with the Germans that he might lead them into a trap, into British or American or even French hands.

"That night David began a long journey, a journey he has not even finished today. It took him four weeks to reach the Spanish border. There he had to wait more weeks. It seemed he had to travel all over France. Sometimes he thought he was going right back from where he had started, to the woods and the little church, so round about was the route. He could use only the back roads, the highways being too dangerous. His travels were hard. He lost many, many pounds. Sometimes he slept in ditches or even sewers. When he travelled he wore his wooden shoes around his neck on a string and pedalled in his sock feet. When his socks wore out an old woman gave him those of her grandson, a prisoner in Germany.

"He thinks that Mr. Z must have bribed the Spanish guards because, after a long wait and for no reason he could understand, he was allowed into that country and he had no trouble in crossing it. He had more trouble getting into Portugal, but from here his countrymen could help. They finally arranged that he should cross the border.

"In Lisbon, his own government supplied him with an air force uniform. They sent him another bar for his Distinguished Service Cross for the two Messerschmitts he had shot down. Then his orders came through and they surprised him very much. He was told not to return to England but to take the Clipper to the United States on an entirely new mission."

"Oh, Father, are you David?" Barney broke in on his father's story.

Flight Lieutenant Morrison swallowed. He picked up his cap and examined it inside.

Barney's mother was squeezing his hand. "How did you guess?" she asked.

"Was it you, Mr. Morrison?" the children chorused.

"Oh, it was just a fellow named David," he answered.

"Oh, David, tell the class. They want to know it from you," Mrs. Morrison said.

"It was you, wasn't it?" Barney challenged flatly.

"Your mother has just said it was," his father answered softly. "I'm lucky, you know. Only a couple of weeks ago I was still trying to get out of Spain."

The flight lieutenant had to show his medal and the new bar. There was something else he had to show, too.

"Where's the Iron Cross?" Anthony asked. But he didn't sound "smart." It was just that he wanted to see it.

"Right here in my pocket. Take a look. It's the single thing I was able to bring out of France." Flight Lieutenant Morrison took the German badge out of his pocket and passed it to Anthony.

CHAPTER TWENTY-FIVE

"You mean you're going to stay in this country? You're not going back to England?" Barney could hardly believe his father's words. They seemed so wonderful they surely couldn't be true.

"That's it. That's right. For a while, anyway. Perhaps until after the war," his father answered.

They were back at Grandma's. She had been as surprised as Barney. His father hadn't stopped to see her. He had been so anxious to see Barney that he had his taxi go from the airport to school. It had been lucky that Mother and Aunt Kitty had arrived first, for he would have been impatient if he'd had to wait for them.

Barney and his father were on the porch swing. His mother and Aunt Kitty were helping Grandma and Blanche get dinner and fix the bedrooms.

"Will I live in St. Louis, too?" Until now, Barney had been afraid to ask the question he most wanted answered. He waited until he could bring himself to ask it because he was afraid the answer might be "No."

"That's it. We'll live in St. Louis." His father sounded different from Uncle Frank or Mr. Kent or from anyone else Barney knew.

"Me, too?" He had to be sure.

"Why, of course! I realize I haven't been much of a father, Barney, but I'll try to do better after this."

"I thought you'd forgotten me. I thought you would have written if you'd remembered."

Barnacle jumped up onto the swing and Barney's father began stroking him. He didn't say anything for a long time. He seemed more interested in the kitten than in anything else.

Barney could now understand why his father hadn't written during all those weeks in France and Spain. Even Mother hadn't heard from him. Barney felt terribly sorry. She must have been worried to death.

"Will Mother be with us in St. Louis?" he asked.

"To be sure. You don't suppose she'd stay in Washington with the two of us in St. Louis, do you?"

Barney felt glad about this, that his father included him in making Mother want to be with them. He knew it wasn't so much for his sake as for his father's that she was going to move, because she'd stayed in Washington when he was in Pittsburgh. He didn't say anything about this, only, "What about her war job?"

"She was able to get transferred to St. Louis. The same way your Aunt Kitty got transferred here."

"Is Aunt Kitty going to work here now?" Barney found this very good news indeed. "That'll be wonderful—for Grandma," he added when he realized he wouldn't be here but in St. Louis.

"That's why she's here today," his father said. "Her transfer was very sudden. She didn't even get a day's notice."

Just then Aunt Kitty came out with a plate of cookies.

"Did your colonel really let you come? The chicken colonel?"

"Barney remembers everything," Aunt Kitty laughed. "Yes, the colonel let me come. He couldn't help himself. He got transferred here, too. So did our whole department. It was awfully sudden though. On Saturday Colonel Miller told me to return to Washington. Today he sent me back to Pittsburgh. Something's going to happen in Europe very soon or I miss my guess."

"What about Margie Baines?"

"Margie got a break, too. When the rest of us got sent here they didn't need her. She'll just go to another office in Washington. She can be married now."

"No more school, Barney." Aunt Kitty changed the subject. "Your mother has just decided that with only four more days you can stop right now."

No more school! Funny about school. Now that he was leaving he was beginning to like Anthony and some of the girls. Maybe they weren't so bad. Anthony hadn't been a bit smarty about his dad. And what a way to end school! No one had believed his father was a flier. And then Dad just walked into the schoolroom and they had to believe it. Not only that, his father told them about his last air battle and how he was shot down and how he escaped. When he had finished, everyone in the schoolroom crowded around to examine his medals, his stripes and badges. They even admired Barney's own R.A.F. pin. There wasn't one in the room who wouldn't have liked to have a pin like that, to have a father like his.

Grandma had telephoned the news about Barney's father to Grandpa and Uncle Frank and they came home early from work. The whole family gathered in the living room before dinner. They were all talking at once, all asking questions of Barney's father. They wanted to know about the American Army in England and in Italy, and about our fliers and the R.A.F.

Father answered them as well as he could. He told them anything he knew for sure about the Americans and what they were doing and a lot of other things besides. He told of his own sweeps and of some of the brave fliers he had known. He told them he never meant to fly again unless he could carry chewing gum.

Then they had to hear about Aunt Kitty and her change in plans. Again they all seemed to be talking at once.

"Mother can't complain that she's all alone in this house," Barney heard Uncle Frank telling Aunt Kitty.

"Barney certainly fixed that," Aunt Kitty answered. "First he got you back and now me. I haven't said anything about this before, but something Barney said may have started this. When I phoned on Saturday I made a suggestion. It's being carried out."

"Your department being moved here?" Uncle Frank asked.

"Well, there was a danger of duplication I pointed out. The same work would be done in two offices. Some of the people in the Pittsburgh office will be promoted to better jobs.",

"Barney certainly fixed things," Uncle Frank went on. "He hired a couple of servants."

"And he imported a family of cats." Grandpa was passing cigars and had overheard what they were saying.

"And I was all alone in this big house." Grandma was talking to Barney's father. She hadn't heard the others.

"Not any more," the rest of them said together, even Grandpa joining in. "Not after Barney took hold," Uncle Frank added.

Outside Barnacle was meowing. Barney went out to see why. Across the street, Mr. Kent was mowing his lawn. It would only take a minute to tell Mr. Kent the good news about his father.

"Hi ya, Mr. Kent." He was across the street with Barnacle digging his sharp little claws into the threads of his pullover.

"Hi ya, Barney," Mr. Kent answered.

"You'd better come over to my house, Mr. Kent. My father's there. He just escaped from the Germans."

"Your father? He's here? No, you don't mean it?" For the first time since he'd known him, Barney had said something that really interested Mr. Kent. Always in the past, his tones had been low and even. He'd always been polite but he had sounded as if he didn't very much care.

"He was shot down over France. A French boy my age saved him. He hid in a church and then in a coal mine. He's an R.A.F. flier, you know."

"So he really *is* an R.A.F. flier," Mr. Kent mused. Barney knew he hadn't ever before believed him.

"You'd better come over and meet him. Aunt Kitty's home, too."

"Your Aunt Kitty? Is she really? Why, how did that happen?" From the way he spoke, Barney felt Mr. Kent was even more interested in Aunt Kitty than in what he had just said about his father. But that just didn't make sense. That couldn't be.

"Sure. Come on over. Come and meet my father," he invited.

"I'd like to do that, Barney. Do you suppose it will be all right if I come after dinner? Would your Aunt Kitty mind?"

"Aunt Kitty? I don't know why she would. I don't know why anyone would mind if you came to see my father."

"I'd like to see her, too. If she wouldn't mind."

"You don't understand, Mr. Kent. My *father's* home

from Europe. He was shot down in France. He escaped."

"Yes, yes. I know. I do believe you; I believe he's an R.A.F. pilot."

"Well, you keep talking about Aunt Kitty," Barney answered. Then an idea flashed like an electric sign. "Say, Mr. Kent, you aren't thinking of marrying her, are you?"

"Do you think she'd have me?"

"Well, I don't know. Maybe she would. About a thing like that there's no telling. You could ask her." Barney seemed doubtful.

"I'm going to do that." Mr. Kent spoke with determination. "Say, Barney, will you do something for me? Will you tell your Aunt Kitty I'll be over tonight. Then if she makes a face or if she says anything that makes you think she'd rather I didn't, will you come back and tell me?"

"Sure, Mr. Kent. But you've got to meet my father."

"Yes, of course. But not tonight if your Aunt Kitty doesn't want me to come."

"Well, so long, Mr. Kent. I'll be seeing you."

Up the street, Angelo was cutting the hedge next to Mr. Day's. Mr. Day was on the porch talking to him.

"Hi ya, Angelo. Hi ya, Mr. Day. My father's here. He's escaped from the Germans. You'd better come to see him."

Henry, the paper boy, was hurling papers onto porches. "Hi ya, Henry. My father's home from Europe."

"Paper, paper," Henry started yelling. "Barney's father's here. He's escaped from the Germans. Paper, paper."

*　　*　　*　　*

When Barney awoke the next morning he could hear the radio. He jumped out of bed and ran to find his father. His father and all the family were dressed and seated in a circle around the radio.

"It's D-Day, Barney. Our troops have landed in France," his father said.

"Does it mean you'll have to go back?" he asked.

"It isn't my kind of show, Barney. It's one I hate to miss, but if I were in it I should still be flying from an English base."

"Does it mean the Germans are licked in France?" Barney asked.

"We hope they soon will be. We hope they'll be driven out, that the fine French people will be free as we English and you Americans."

"And Father Ferrand and Louis and Gervais?"

"Let's hope they are no longer in danger of being found out by the Germans. Their village is in Northern France and may soon be liberated. Soon I can send back the francs that Messieurs X, Y and Z gave me. Soon, perhaps, I can send Father Ferrand money for a new statue of St. Denis."

"And Gervais?"

"I've been thinking of Gervais and Henri. Henri, I believe, Father Ferrand had picked to lead the Germans into a trap. It's Gervais and Henri and the ones like them who are going to decide whether this invasion will succeed."

"Little children," Aunt Kitty said.

"Mere kids," Uncle Frank added.

"Bits of boys no bigger than Barney." His mother spoke.

"Men, though, in loving their country, in loving freedom," Grandma surprisingly said.

It was Grandpa who put into words what they were all thinking.

"These little children have learned to know the cost of freedom. So they value it as perhaps no other children in the world have ever valued freedom. They will guard it. With the lesson they have learned they will make sure it will never be in such danger again. It's their world, anyway. They are the ones who will run it. We can be quite sure they will make a better job of running it than we have."

THE END